ALASKAN MOUNTAIN MURDER

SARAH VARLAND

LOVE INSPIRED SUSPENSE
INSPIRATIONAL ROMANCE

LOVE INSPIRED® SUSPENSE
INSPIRATIONAL ROMANCE

Recycling programs for this product may not exist in your area.

ISBN-13: 978-1-335-40281-3

Alaskan Mountain Murder

Copyright © 2020 by Sarah Varland

This edition published by arrangement with Harlequin Books S.A.

For questions and comments about the quality of this book, please contact us at CustomerService@Harlequin.com.

Love Inspired
22 Adelaide St. West, 40th Floor
Toronto, Ontario M5H 4E3, Canada
www.Harlequin.com

Printed in U.S.A.

The gunshot scattered dust at her feet.

"Get down!" She tackled her son. Their son.

"Was that a gun, Mommy?"

That was a question she never thought she'd have to answer. Her heart beat a terrified rhythm and then there was a weight on top of her. Jake. He'd dived on her to shelter them.

Cassie needed time to figure out what that meant, but the gunshots continued.

"What do we do?" she asked Jake. Why had she assumed they'd be safe from the killers here? Maybe because coming after them didn't make sense. Unless they'd come close to finding something. But what?

Finally, the shots stopped and stillness returned to the woods.

The boy started to cry and Jake calmed him. Then he turned to her. "We need to move."

At Jake's word, they started hiking, faster, and Cassie kept vigil, looking for a threat she knew was out there somewhere.

Someone had shot at them today and could still be watching even now.

And she was their prime target.

Sarah Varland lives in Alaska with her husband, John, their two boys and their dogs. Her passion for books comes from her mom; her love for suspense comes from her dad, who has spent a career in law enforcement. When she's not writing, she's often found dog mushing, hiking, reading, kayaking, drinking coffee or enjoying other Alaskan adventures with her family.

Books by Sarah Varland

Love Inspired Suspense

Visit the Author Profile page at Harlequin.com.

If we confess our sins, he is faithful and just to forgive us our sins, and to cleanse us from all unrighteousness.
−1 John 1:9

To my family. Thank you for everything.

ONE

The sight of the front door hanging open, crooked on its hinges, was the first time Cassie Hawkins let herself consider that something might be really wrong. As she sat in the relative safety of her rental car staring at her aunt's home, she wondered if she should go in this late at night. She'd gotten the phone call as her aunt's next of kin—more like a daughter than a niece after all the years Cassie had lived with her—that she was missing. But it was Alaska, people went missing often in innocent ways that still had them coming home eventually. Hikers got lost. Plans changed and independent Alaskans forgot to tell their friends.

Cassie couldn't say that she'd heard of many disappearances beginning with open house doors that ended well. She swallowed hard and started to step out of the car. She had one foot on the Alaskan ground she'd sworn years ago never to return to when she hesitated, climbed back into the vehicle. Was it safe to go inside?

Her gaze went to the seat behind her, where six-year-old Will was dozing soundly, his cheek pressed against the headrest of his high-back booster. He'd fallen asleep just after they'd left the airport in Anchorage, before they'd headed south on the Seward Highway. She'd driven the familiar curving road in silence, appreciating the sweeping views of Turnagain Arm and the mountains that guarded it, even as her chest tightened at the idea of being this close to Raven Pass. To home.

To Jake Stone.

She exhaled a long breath, all the weariness of the last few days tangled up in it. She couldn't leave Will in the car, not when no one seemed to have a good answer for how her aunt had disappeared. If there was foul play involved—and the state of the door on the house made her uncomfortable—she couldn't risk her son. He was all she had.

That and an overwhelming sense of guilt that her former fiancé had no idea he existed.

Her stomach turned and she swallowed hard. She should go to Jake's house first, before she did anything else, before she let Will out of the car and small-town tongues started talking. She hadn't meant to keep Will from him, not really. But as she'd let more time pass without having that necessary conversation—one that was too important for a phone call but that she'd never worked up the courage to have in person—it had gotten more difficult to face the inevitable.

He needed to know.

Cassie climbed back into the car, shut the door and pulled out of the driveway, checked her rearview as she navigated back onto Raven Pass's main road.

There. Behind her on the side of the road. Hadn't she seen that gray car before? It had been behind her on the highway earlier. And hadn't they stopped for gas when she'd stopped in Girdwood, just fifteen miles or so back?

And now they were in Raven Pass too, right here near her aunt's house?

She took a deep breath, felt her heartbeat slow and steady as she braced herself for a crisis. Cassie had many faults, she was well aware of them, but when something went wrong, it was like her mind buckled down, readied itself for battle.

It was what had made her want to be a doctor all those years ago, the suggestion she could use that skill to help people.

If only she'd gotten the chance. But life was too short to waste on regrets. And besides, she wouldn't trade Will for all the degrees and dreams in the world. Jake would tell her that God had a way of redeeming situations and turning challenges into blessings. He'd always said things like that when they were dating, spoken of God like He cared about her.

Cassie? She'd never been sure.

Out on the road, she put the rental car back in Drive and headed forward, toward Jake's house, her eyes flitting between the road in front of her and the rearview mirror.

The gray car followed.

Cassie swallowed hard, increased her speed as the other car did the same. She led the car back out of town, onto the Seward Highway. Her eyes went once again to Will's sleeping face. She'd do anything to protect her son. But what if it wasn't enough? She couldn't lose him.

Please, God. She fumbled with the words. Jake had tried to introduce her to the God he loved, but Cassie had never quite understood. How could Jake talk to God as though He were right there, a friend, and not a far-off Being who created the world and existed somewhere far away.

Still, it was worth a try. Hopefully that would count for something and if He was there as Jake insisted He was, He'd help her somehow.

The car edged closer and Cassie reached for her cell, which was sitting on the dashboard. She'd not bothered to sync it to the rental's Bluetooth system when she'd picked up the vehicle. Keeping her eyes on the road, she wrapped her fingers around the slick, cool phone.

It slid from her hand to the floorboard. She glanced down, looked back up again in time to swerve back right and miss the truck she'd almost hit head-on in the attempt to get her phone.

She'd have to call the police later. Right now she was on her own.

There were no turnoffs that were a good place for losing the tail, not unless she could drive around Girdwood and lose him in one of the neighborhoods filled with houses and vacation cabins.

Otherwise her option was to drive on the dangerous Seward Highway all the way back to Anchorage with him on her tail. Some of the curves of the road hugged rock cliffs on one side, where the mountain itself had been blasted to build the highway, and the ocean on the other. It wasn't a risk she was willing to take.

She'd have to try to lose him. Cassie turned right onto the Alyeska Highway, a generous name for the two-lane road that led to the resort town of Girdwood, the town nearest to Raven Pass, and pushed the engine as far over the limit as she dared. Drawing someone's attention with her speed could help her, but on the other hand, this was a town where many people walked and rode their bikes and she didn't want to risk hitting anyone. Even this late at night people could be out, though it seemed hardly anyone was.

No matter how many turns down obscure neighborhood roads she made, Cassie couldn't shake the tail. And she couldn't make out any of the driver's facial features either.

This had to stop. Every minute that swept by her heart beat faster and she felt her body temperature rising. She only had so much longer to be able to hold it together.

She'd go back to Raven Pass, to the police department there. She should have thought of that in the first place. She'd just been so determined to try to lose her tail. All she could do was try to make better decisions now, and that started with finding a police department. Since Girdwood had no department of its own, Raven Pass was her best bet. She needed to go back.

Pressing the gas pedal hard and gripping the steering wheel like she had NASCAR aspirations, she drove hard, back toward town.

She'd just made it past the Welcome to Raven Pass sign when the gray car accelerated, and Cassie hit the gas but braced herself for impact in case she'd reacted too slowly.

She had.

The crash was an instant of crunching metal and pain in Cassie's head, and the car threatened to spin out as she fought the wheel for control. After seconds that seemed like minutes, she won, and the sedan slowed to a stop on the side of the road. She was grateful it hadn't been a hard enough jolt for the airbag to deploy. There were no other vehicles in sight, probably because she'd had the brilliant idea to come to town right after her flight got in, which meant it was just past midnight, not exactly the prime traffic time of day. She should have spent the night at a hotel in Anchorage and waited until day to head to Raven Pass, but then how could she have known she'd be followed? Run off the road?

Cassie twisted in her seat to look in the back, thankful to see that Will looked uninjured. He was awake, his eyes wide, his cheek still marked with wrinkles from being pressed against the booster seat, an image that turned her heart upside down with sheer love.

She had to keep him safe.

"Did we get in a wreck?" he asked, his eyes wide, voice wavering.

If only she had the time to reassure him fully, but the door of the gray car behind them was opening. And she had no choice but to run.

"Listen, baby," she said as she unbuckled his seat, "when I open your door, I need you to run as fast as you can, okay? We're going into the trees there." She motioned with her finger toward the dark spruce woods. Memories fought to surface—hiking the woods with Jake, finding places where they could talk—and not talk—without interruption. Would the memories always feel so suffocating? She'd felt numb in Florida. Up here though, she felt everything as deeply as ever. Every ounce of love she'd ever had for him, the regret at her rash decision to leave town.

But time couldn't be turned back.

And right now her focus was keeping her son—and herself—safe.

"Ready?" she asked him, taking a deep breath.

"Ready, Mom." His little voice was confident. Trusting.

Please, God, don't let me let him down. She tried another prayer, remembering the way Jake had talked to God.

"Go!" She threw her door open, then quickly yanked his wide, and they both took off into the woods.

"Hey!" her attacker yelled—the voice was male, but she didn't notice any more than that in her hurry to escape—but they didn't turn around. Instead they ran, straight for the path Cassie remembered, which would take them to town—where it came out she couldn't remember, but someone would help her. It was a tight-knit community, where you could count on your neighbors.

And hopefully find safety.

They ran until Will started to lag and then Cassie picked him up, his head resting on her shoulder as she pushed herself as fast as she could with a sixty-pound boy draped across her.

Ignoring the burn in her legs, the sharp pain in her lungs as she gasped for breath after breath, exhaustion and adrenaline fighting for dominance, Cassie closed the gap between where she was and town, glancing back now and then to see if she was being pursued. Once she'd seen someone, large and tall, dressed in dark clothes with a ski mask, and since then she'd pushed her pace harder. As the woods grew thicker, her pace slowed by necessity, and she stepped off the trail, staying close enough to it that she knew where she was—at least she thought so—but hoping her pursuer wouldn't be able to find her, even if he did catch up. The path she made through the trees was tight but it worked, twisting around large stalks of the thorn-laden devil's club plant.

The darkness of the woods grew thicker as she ap-

proached Fourteen-Mile River. The main trail had a
bridge, but since she'd been avoiding that path, she'd
have to run through the river and soak her legs. Better
than being caught by whoever had been after her.

She splashed through the water, the icy cold like a
thousand needles in her skin as she ran. Not far now,
maybe a quarter of a mile till the path would end. She
just needed to figure out where she was going to come
out in relation to town, and plot her path to the police
station. Or just find the first house and ask for help and
a phone to call the police. She'd decide which when she
got there.

Cassie glanced back one more time, saw the tall man
dressed in dirty jeans and a jacket, a ski mask on his
head. He was closer now than he had been, and she could
see a large gun in his right hand.

Any doubts about whether she was justified in running, about whether or not her aunt had disappeared
naturally, fled from her mind.

Something was going on in Raven Pass, something
that had put her aunt, and now Cassie and her son, in
danger.

She was fueled by adrenaline now, keenly aware that
it would fade soon and then she'd be at his mercy.

Cassie was determined not to let it happen. So she
kept running, pushing through the last bit of crowded
forest onto a gravel path, lifting her eyes to look straight
at the house in front of her.

Light green with dark green trim. An octagonal window above the front door on the second story.

She'd run straight to Jake Stone's old house. Just like
old times, like she could still count on him to sweep her

into his solid arms and tell her everything was going to be okay.

Those days were long gone, and Jake had surely moved out of his parents' old home, but she needed help, and needed it now. She felt convinced whoever was after her wouldn't hesitate to snatch her even from here, on the edges of town where someone could see. Why else would he have worn a mask to conceal his identity?

She needed to get inside that house. Call the police. Sort this out.

So she didn't hesitate any longer. She sprinted across the street, and threw open the door, just like she would have without hesitation seven years ago—when the Stones had treated her like part of the family, when it had been assumed she and Jake would follow through on their engagement and maybe one day live in this adorable house in Raven Pass.

Back before everything blew up. And Cassie had been left holding the fuse.

She could only pray his parents had forgiven her, but even if they hadn't, they were decent people. They would keep her safe, she was sure of it.

She shut the door hard behind her and locked it, then set a wide-eyed Will down beside her.

"Are we okay, Mom?" he asked in a shaky voice.

"We will be, sweetie. Stay right here, okay?" Cassie moved toward the kitchen, hoping they still had a landline.

And ran straight into a solid person. Tall. Much, much too solid to be Jake's dad.

And found herself looking right into the sky blue eyes of the man whose heart she'd broken seven years ago. Jake Stone.

* * *

"Cassie?"

Jake barely managed to sputter out her name, the one he hadn't spoken aloud more than a handful of times in years. He'd imagined what it would be like to see her once more, maybe even let himself have the slightest daydream about her being against his chest like this again.

But deep down he'd known the latter would never happen, and the former probably wouldn't either. He'd heard her aunt was missing and he'd let himself wonder if Cassie would come but hadn't really thought she would.

Now she was in his house. And there was a little boy standing beside her.

A little boy who looked… Jake swallowed hard. Seven? Six?

She hadn't said a word to him about the boy yet, but Jake saw his eyes in the boy's face, saw his own childhood expression mirrored.

"What are you doing here?" He put his hands on her upper arms, gently, and stepped back, looked her over. Her brown-sugar hair was tangled around her face, which was red, like she'd been exercising.

"My aunt is gone. I'm in town because of that, but when I went to her house the door was open and I don't know why. Someone followed me here." Cassie turned quickly, looked behind her though nothing was back there.

"And you ran here…?"

"I didn't come here on purpose." Her cheeks reddened further. "Listen." She cleared her throat, her tone switching to the all-business one she used when she was uncomfortable. "I'm sorry to have bothered you, but I went to my aunt's house and the door was open, and there was a car and they followed me and ran me off the road..." She glanced back again. "They chased me through the woods, even through Fourteen-Mile River when I crossed it. I needed to get help and this was the first house I saw. I'm sorry, but please. Don't send us away yet, not until the police come."

Jake felt his defenses rise, his shoulders tense. She'd hurt him, sure, probably more than anyone realized. He glanced at the small boy beside her who still hadn't said a word. Swallowed hard. Either way, this was another layer to the hurt. Had she cheated on him? Or...

It wasn't outside the realm of possibility that they could have made a son together. Jake had had good intentions, had his standards and his plans to wait until they were married but it had grown harder and he hadn't resisted temptation as well as he should have.

Cassie didn't share his level of faith, and had said she loved him and that was what had mattered. But still, whether she believed in God or not, it had been his job to keep their relationship on track. He'd failed her.

Had that been the beginning of the end?

"Jake?" Her nervousness was displayed across her features.

What kind of cruel person did she think he was to wonder if he would send her away while she was in so much danger? Especially when she had her son with her. If anything, with the way he was feeling right now, it would be a struggle to let her leave.

Not that she needed to know that. No, she'd lost the right to know his innermost feelings and thoughts when she'd left him and Raven Pass in the dust years ago. Besides, the first thing he needed to do was call the police. He slipped the cell phone out of his pocket, dialed 911 and reported the incident as Cassie had told it to him. He thought he noticed her relax a little from her place beside him, but she still looked behind her several times a minute, her grip on the boy's shoulders seeming to get tighter. The boy squirmed. "You're squashing my bones, Mom," he finally said in a dry tone.

"Sorry, sweetheart." She looked down at him, squeezed him against her in a hug. Cassie as a mom. The sight was a gut punch. She seemed good at it, comfortable with motherhood. He'd always known she would be, despite her doubts because of her own upbringing.

"Do you have any kind of description of the guy who was after you? That might help the police." Why that was the question that came out when he had a hundred others overwhelming his mind, he didn't know, but she looked relieved. Because she wanted to think through the trauma she'd just been through and start to process it? Or because she was glad he hadn't tried to steer the conversation to anything personal?

She shook her head. "It was a man, probably six feet or taller. But he had a ski mask on, so I don't know anything about his appearance beyond that."

This wasn't a spur-of-the-moment crime then. He'd been prepared. Had he been intending to snatch Cassie? Kill her? Or had it just been his plan to watch her and then something had triggered him to go after her?

After them? Did her would-be attacker know she had a son?

"Wait, did you say your aunt's door was busted open?" He frowned. He'd been over there the day of her disappearance with the Raven Pass Search and Rescue Team, of which he was a part, and her house had been in pristine condition, just as she'd left it, with the exception of the few odd things they usually found when people disappeared or died suddenly—a cereal bowl in the sink, a glass on the counter, signs of a life paused midstream.

"Yes. I knew she disappeared, but I was led to believe it could have been accidental, not...whatever this is." Cassie shook her head and Jake watched as the frown between her brows deepened, small wrinkles on her forehead pinching as her expression darkened.

"Her door wasn't open the other day," he said, wondering as the words left his mouth if this was the best way to let her know that he was involved in the search for her aunt. Too late now, he guessed. Cassie wouldn't have appreciated being danced lightly around anyway. She'd always insisted she could handle the truth straight. And maybe she could. Jake had tried that once, had told her the dreams he'd had of the two of them, the family he imagined, and though they'd been engaged, she just left. Had she not wanted kids? Had the future overwhelmed her so much? Or had it been him?

He didn't know, but the irony was inescapable and cutting. She'd gone. Had a kid without him.

It was a knife in his chest, one he felt every time he took a breath.

"Why were you there?"

May as well answer her. "I'm on a search-and-rescue team and we've been looking for your aunt."

"I thought the police were looking?" Her eyebrows were raised.

"They are. It's not unusual for them to utilize our resources out here. It's rough country, you know that. Teamwork helps people get home safely."

"Search and rescue? What happened to med school?"

The knock at the door announced the police officer's arrival, and Jake was spared at least that question. This conversation was exhausting to have with the woman he'd loved enough to want to spend the rest of his life with, now that she was acting like a virtual stranger. But one who was intensely familiar with his past.

Was his past.

Jake moved to the door but noticed Cassie had tensed, her shoulders edging toward her ears as she pulled the boy closer to her again. "Cassie, it's the police, okay?" he said once he'd confirmed the assumption through the peephole in the door. "You don't have to worry right now."

She swallowed hard and he watched her light green eyes flick glances around the room. She'd delivered her account of what had happened with remarkable calmness and clarity, but she was rattled, no doubt about it. Seven years ago he would have sat down with her, made her some coffee that was mostly cream, the way she liked it, and then listened while she processed out loud, the way she always did.

But everything between them had changed now and he felt like someone who didn't understand what his next step should be. There was too much between them— had been at one time anyway—for him to be comfortable just sending her off with the police and not seeing her again, not following up at all. Then again, she'd left, hadn't she? Left *him*. Who was to say she wanted him to care anymore, on any level?

He needed to remember to keep ahold of his feelings, remind himself that she hadn't come to his house on purpose. It was coincidence, maybe some part of her subconscious at the absolute most. But she didn't want *his* help. Not specifically. That was critical for him to remember.

However, at the same time…they needed to have a conversation. There were two explanations for the boy with her—either he was his father, or she'd betrayed him worse than he'd imagined, being with someone like that so soon after their breakup, or even before. One way or another he needed to know, and he couldn't even wrap his mind around either option being true. But at the moment his main focus was on reporting this to the police and getting together a game plan to make sure Cassie didn't have to have that kind of fear in her eyes again.

The knock came again, more forceful this time, and he hurried to open the door, having confirmed that it was the police.

"Jake. Morning." Levi Wicks was one of the officers Jake knew best, having worked with him on a search-and-rescue case several months back. Of all the officers who could have responded, Levi was the one most likely to welcome Raven Pass Search and Rescue's help.

"Morning, Officer Wicks."

Levi rolled his eyes at him, but Jake wasn't teasing him by using the title, just wanted his friend to know he respected his position and didn't take their friendship for granted.

"Good morning, Jake." The other officer, Christy Ames, smiled at Jake, then looked past him. "Cassie?" Her eyes widened. Jake sometimes forgot that some of his friends now had been *their* friends when he and Cassie were a couple. Raven Pass had grown and changed enough in the years that she'd been gone that he sometimes lost track of how many people had been in high school with them, watched them fall in love and then been around to witness the aftermath of Cassie's departure.

"Hi, Christy." Cassie attempted a small smile.

"You two know each other?" Levi shook his head. "I'm never going to get used to how small towns work."

"We went to high school together," Christy explained, then looked to Jake. "This is the woman you called and told us about who was almost abducted? And you didn't specify *who* it was?"

"I figured you'd find out when you got here." Jake shrugged.

Christy gave a slight shake of her head, then moved toward Cassie. "Rather than have this conversation standing in the entryway, why don't we move to the living room. Sound good to you, Jake?" Christy led the way, having visited his house in high school with Cassie. His parents had left town several years back, choosing to move deep into the Alaska wilderness near Anaktuvuk Pass. Most people his parents' age left Alaska for the warmth of the south. They didn't opt for *more* Alaska when they moved, but that was just his parents. If he could be half the adventurers they'd always been, he'd be happy with his life.

Without consciously meaning to, he looked at Cassie. At the little boy beside her.

Once upon a time, he'd assumed being happy had meant being with Cassie. Funny how dreams changed. Some came true and some disappeared quicker than frost on a late spring morning.

All he could do was move on. Just like he'd been trying to do for years.

Only to end up where he was today, with Cassie back in his house, tangling up his thoughts and feelings, and making him feel like no time had passed at all.

TWO

Both officers, Levi Wicks and Christy—who Cassie was having a hard time believing was the same person she'd known in high school—were kind in their questioning, but Cassie still felt as if her head were spinning. If only she'd gotten a better look at the man. She'd done everything she could, they assured her, and while Cassie knew in her head that their words were true, she still couldn't quite shake her guilt for putting Will in that situation. She'd had no inkling they'd be facing this kind of threat in Alaska, or she'd have... What? She had friends in Florida, ones she'd trust with Will, but not for such a long period of time. So she'd had no choice but to bring him with her. He was in the room with them now, hearing things no six-year-old should about danger, but he was playing a *How to Train Your Dragon* game on her phone, which Officer Wicks had brought since they'd stopped by the scene of Cassie's accident on their way, so she could only hope his little mind was full of Night Fury dragons and not this conversation she was having with the police.

"We've been working this as a typical missing persons case, but no one had reported the damage to the house that you've just told us about," Officer Wicks told her. He glanced down at his phone. "Excuse me just a minute."

He stood and walked to another room to take the call, then came back.

"That was one of the other officers confirming what you said about the door and telling me about the rest of the house."

"Was it more than just the front door?" Cassie asked, having not gotten far enough in her thoughts to wonder about that.

"Yes, the house has damage in several rooms. The office and the bedroom look like a tornado blew through, but jewelry and electronics are still there, so it's not a random break-in."

"Which means we need to change the way we are running the search also," Jake said. "We've been looking for her, but the assumption was that there was a good chance it was a hike that went wrong."

Did that change how the search-and-rescue team worked? Cassie wouldn't have guessed so, but then again she didn't know much about that kind of work.

Office Wicks spoke again. "The sooner you can meet with your team and brief them, the better. They need to know to be on guard also, in case any evidence they might uncover could make them targets."

Jake nodded. He was still worried; she knew by the way the corners of his eyes crinkled, the blue in them shadowed ever so slightly. He looked at Christy, who seemed to understand better than Cassie what was bothering him. A fact which bothered Cassie far more than it should have when this was a man she'd given up every claim to years ago. And had driven a bigger wedge between them by keeping Will a secret, something they hadn't talked about yet but would need to. Jake had been kind to Will, calm in his presence. Had he guessed his age? Could he see a resemblance and know it was his son? Cassie didn't know—she'd never considered how any of this would play out, at least not in any realistic sort of way. Or did Jake think she'd been unfaithful?

That idea hurt. She would have never been untrue to him. She'd loved him, completely.

"Cassie, you need to stay with someone." Christy didn't bother softening the words with any kind of preamble.

"I had been planning to stay at my aunt's house." She scooted forward to the edge of the couch she'd been sitting on. "If you're done with me now, I'll just head that way." Because if the police were finished taking her statement, then they'd be leaving soon, and no way was she sitting here alone with Jake. The conversation they needed to have could be done…another time. Right? She'd already been in his house too long and she couldn't deal with the growing tangle of confusing feelings inside her, the guilt tormenting her.

God, forgive me. I should have told him about Will sooner.

A third prayer to a God she had never been sure existed. Cassie wanted to sort those feelings out later, figure out why it was starting to feel natural. She wished she could talk to Jake about it.

Looking over at him, his broad shoulders that had always been there to help her carry any burden she'd faced, his clear glacier-blue eyes that had never once lied to her, it was hard to remember why she'd left.

And then she remembered it had never been Jake. He'd never been the reason.

It had been all her.

They'd had their future planned. She'd doodled her first name and his last name all over her wedding notebook, had filled it with ideas for their day. And then somewhere along the line she'd realized she wasn't just planning a wedding, wasn't just falling in love. She was about to spend the rest of her life as someone's wife. *Jake's* wife. She'd been raised by just her dad—well, he'd had some help from his sister, her aunt who was now missing—after her mom had left him when she was two. He'd done an amazing job and had tried to give her everything she could ever need, but she had still never quite felt like part of a *family*. Not the kind like Jake had. Maybe that was why she'd gravitated toward him in the first place, his idyllic life, though as she'd gotten to know him and had started a relationship with him, she'd fallen head over heels for the man himself.

And then she'd realized that as much as she wanted a family, she had her mom's DNA, her blood in her veins and…what if she turned out like her? Left Jake and some sweet blue-eyed baby? Besides that, here in town people would have expected her to be his support as his wife. She'd had dreams of her own, wanted to be a doctor just like Jake had. She couldn't reconcile her dreams with being a traditional wife, and she'd wondered if that's what had sent her mother away, wanting more, feeling trapped, even by love. She'd panicked. So she'd left, given them both space to pursue their dreams.

But she'd left without explanation, and she could only assume she'd broken his heart. She'd certainly broken her own.

They were all staring at her, she realized after a minute or so of being lost in her own personal memory lane.

"Would you be open to the possibility of staying somewhere else?" Officer Wicks asked, and she guessed she should be thankful he was asking and not ordering her. Not that police were allowed to order people around for no reason, but she understood the fact that she was risking her safety by going back to her aunt's house.

But what other options did she have?

"If you both feel it's necessary, I can consider something. I certainly don't want to endanger Will." She addressed her comment to the officers, hoping that despite what she'd heard about Jake getting his *team* involved, whatever that meant, that he'd stay out of this particular conversation.

"Then it's settled, you'll stay here," Jake spoke up.

She felt the blood rush to her head and a wave of dizzy panic hit her. Cassie swallowed hard, blinked the feeling away. "I'm not staying…"

"All nice and professional. My parents turned the upstairs into sort of apartments. You'll have privacy but I'll be close by. The two of you will be safe there."

Cassie opened her mouth to argue. Closed it again.

Seeming satisfied, Christy and Officer Wicks both stood and moved toward the door before Cassie could decide what to say, how to protest. She wanted to stop them, demand that they stay, but what, was she afraid to be alone with him? Surely not. Even if her…feelings hadn't dissipated over the last decade, she was an adult. She knew when relationships weren't healthy, and she wasn't good enough for Jake. That should keep her away from him no matter how much looking at him, being in the same room with him, made her wish she could forget all the reasons she'd ended it in the first place.

And she would stay away from him.

Even if it was going to be infinitely harder to do while living in his house.

"Remember, if you think of anything else that could help, description-wise, give us a call anytime, okay?" Christy handed her a business card, which Cassie took as she felt herself nod. Then she stuck the card in her back pocket.

"Thanks for coming out," Jake said, then the two officers left. Jake shut the door behind them.

And it was just the three of them. Mother. Son.

And Father who didn't know he was one.

"We need to talk." Jake could feel the charge in the air between them, a thousand levels of awkward and the invisible scarring that came from being so close to someone in the past only to have your shared life ripped in two and not see her again for seven years.

And she came back in danger. Needing your help.

And with a son.

"We do." She agreed before he could follow his train of thought any further. His heart skipped a beat. Nodded. He waited for her to start, looked over at the kid who was still playing on the cell phone.

"Will?" Cassie waited until he looked up to continue. "We're going to stay here. I...I knew Jake when I lived here before."

He nodded. "Okay."

"We're going to stay here, okay?" she repeated, as if stalling for time.

"Because the guy was chasing us earlier?"

"Yeah. It's safer if we aren't alone, all right, bud?" She moved closer to him, pulled him into a hug and kissed the top of his head, then drew a breath.

"Maybe we could stream a movie for him?" she asked Jake. Jake nodded, understanding that whatever way this was going, Will didn't need to hear the conversation. He turned Netflix on, scrolled through the kid options until he got to one about dragons, at which point the kid re-acted enthusiastically and he offered him his Bluetooth headphones. There, they were now functionally alone. At least enough to finish this conversation.

"So..." Cassie trailed off as she took a seat on one of the chairs, her shoulders tense as she perched on the edge of the cushion. She wasn't in any better shape than Jake was. He took a deep breath, tried to convince his shoulders to un-hunch.

"Please don't do that, Cassie. Just..." Just what? He couldn't very well tell her to spit it out, not when it was something this important.

"Sorry. I'm sorry. You need to know." She took a breath.

Jake braced himself the best he could.

"He's yours, Jake."

He'd have said five minutes ago he was prepared to hear either, but there was no way a man could process this well. At least not that Jake could figure out. He stood, walked across the room. Back to the chair. Across.

Run. He could go running. His feet on the trail through the woods, using his body and his mind to the limit would help, but he couldn't leave Cassie right now. Or Will.

His son.

Air. He needed air. He walked to the kitchen, as far

from Cassie and Will in the living room as he dared to go without feeling like he was putting their safety in jeopardy.

After a few minutes he started back toward her. "Cassie…" He trailed off. What was there to ask? He let his eyes go back to Will, took in his features with the knowledge that he was his. *His son.* Again, the words echoed in the hollow spaces inside him, the ones Cassie's leaving had caused. He had more family? Someone counting on him?

He opened his mouth to ask her another question when someone knocked on the door. He watched her shoulders tense.

"I'll answer." He stepped toward it, willing it to be someone who'd go away quickly. He didn't want this conversation interrupted.

THREE

A knock sounded at the door before he could ask whatever question had been on his mind. Cassie sat up straighter, feeling every muscle in her back and shoulders bunch up and ache. Logic told her the man after her wasn't the kind to knock, but the idea of facing him again, or facing anyone unexpectedly, made her tense.

Jake opened the door. Stepped outside. Cassie waited. A girlfriend he wanted to prep for Cassie's sudden reappearance? She hadn't even let herself consider that Jake could be in a relationship, but of course it made sense. Jake was a good man, the kind who deserved a family. One that lived with him, let him be the husband and father he'd always dreamed of being.

He stepped back inside, blew out a breath.

"Someone you need to talk to?" Cassie tried to keep the hurt out of her voice, reminded herself she deserved anything she had to face. She'd made her choices and believed fully that meant she had to live with them.

"They want to talk to both of us actually." He ran a hand through his hair. Cassie had rarely seen him so rattled, but of course the news of his son, her appearance, the threat against her…it made sense it would take a toll.

"Who?"

"My team. The one I mentioned earlier."

"The search-and-rescue team?"

Jake nodded. "They brought dinner." He laughed. "A really late dinner."

Cassie inhaled, held her breath for a second and let it out slowly. "Okay."

"We'll talk more later?"

His eyes, the ones she'd once loved looking into, losing herself in, were unreadable. Maybe it was good for him to have time to process her news, but Cassie needed to know if he forgave her. There was no way to have that conversation when there were people here, and Cassie understood that the case took priority. Assuming they'd come to work, she needed to let them do so.

"Okay," she said again. She nodded. Jake held her gaze for one more second, looking like he was staring straight down to her heart and reading her thoughts the way he used to. But neither of them said anything. Whatever connection they'd had once was severed now.

Wasn't it?

Jake opened the door.

"Two pepperoni pizzas, and one ham and pineapple!" A woman walked in, tall and blond, and held the pizza boxes up with a flourish. Then her eye caught Cassie's.

"You must be Cassie. Awful night you've had." Immediately her expression changed from triumphant and teasing to compassionate. "I'm Piper McAdams."

More people pushed in behind her. Two more women, one with dark hair and skin that was a shade or two more tanned than Cassie's Alaska-toned coloring. And one man who was a little shorter than Jake's six feet three inches, but not by much. He had broad shoulders, like a swimmer.

Piper kept talking as they entered. "This is Adriana Steele—" the woman with dark hair smiled at Cassie "—and Ellie Hardison." The second woman waved at Cassie. She looked like her eyes had a story and Cassie was curious about it. Of course, she was curious about all of these people. None of them was familiar to her, so they must have moved to the area within the last decade. "And Caleb Gaines." Piper pointed to the last man.

Jake took the pizza boxes from Piper and set them on the table. "This is the team, Cassie. Raven Pass Search and Rescue."

Cassie was impressed. Already, less than a minute in their presence, she could tell they all had very different personalities, but they must have figured out some way to work together in their searches. That took a unique kind of teamwork and community and she was excited to see it in action. It was the kind of group that would be interesting to work with. She may not have become a doctor as planned, but she'd gone to school at night, finally gotten her BSN and enjoyed working as a nurse. She knew from those experiences how important good teams were, how working in sync with each other led to good outcomes. Of course, pediatric nursing wasn't quite the same as helping with possible medical emergencies in the backcountry and she knew that, but it would be interesting to try.

If she'd stayed, would she have changed career paths and become a nurse despite her initial plans? Life didn't turn out like you planned; she'd learned that long ago. But seeing the interesting combination of personalities as they all gathered around the table made her wonder what it would be like to work with a team like this.

If she stayed, would they make a place for her?

Cassie slammed that mental door immediately. She was not staying. In fact, she should have been leaving in the next few days, but the police had advised her not to leave the state until they figured out who was after her. Going back to Florida would complicate their case and make it difficult for her to stay safe, even more than it would be here. Not to mention the fact that she wouldn't dream of leaving until she found out what had happened to her aunt.

Just because she wasn't able to leave Raven Pass behind her yet, didn't mean it wasn't inevitable though. She needed to remember she was an outsider here, that she had work and a life waiting for her thousands of miles away. While she was going to be around these good people, so that Jake could keep her safe, maybe she shouldn't offer to help too much or get too close, learn anything that would make her wish for their camaraderie. Something she just couldn't have. She had Will, that was enough. She needed to be thankful for what she had and let go of the what-ifs. There was no sense in dwelling there.

"Cassie, come join us." Piper motioned her over to the pizza, still smiling. "We're going to talk about the search for your aunt and how our game plan for tomorrow is going to change from what it was."

Cassie looked over at the table where Adriana had already unfolded a map and was pointing at something.

"Can you show me where you've already searched?" She'd known this area once, had grown up close to her aunt. Maybe she'd be able to help pinpoint where she could have gone.

She owed it to her aunt to try.

"Sure, come on over."

So Cassie took a deep breath, braced herself the best she could, offered a small smile and joined the group.

And hoped it wasn't going to lead to connections, to friendships that would make leaving them break her heart.

Cassie hadn't slept this badly since she'd left Jake, but every night noise, every sound in the dim Alaska night, seemed to come through the windows and to her ears. Beside her, Will slept soundly. At least that was something. She turned over again, closed her eyes and tried to relax.

No success.

Maybe it wasn't the sounds outside that were keeping her awake at all, but the questions she had. For Jake. For herself. They hadn't been able to talk at all after the rescue team left. It had been too late at night, so they'd both agreed to talk again tomorrow. So that unpleasant conversation was put off for now, but the uncertainty lingered.

Why was Jake working with a rescue team instead of in medicine? He'd explained some, but not nearly all of his reasoning yesterday, she felt. Could she ask him for more details or was that prying? She was unsure of the etiquette when addressing one's former fiancé.

But those weren't the questions that kept her awake, though they were the ones that tugged at her heart, made her wish she could go back in time, and…what? Change something?

The questions keeping her awake were more urgent. Why would someone have abducted her aunt? If that was what had happened, which looked fairly likely given the break-in at her house. Cassie didn't believe in coincidences.

She finally gave up the idea of sleep just past three in the morning and headed down the stairs, back to the main part of the house. She'd seen Jake put leftover pizza into the fridge. Maybe trying to eat a little more would help her sleep.

Down the steps she crept, not wanting to wake Jake.

She heard noise as soon as she made it to the living room and there he was, standing from a chair where he'd apparently been sitting by the fire.

"I'm sorry. I tried to be quiet." She offered the words to ease the awkward feeling she had every time they were alone. Though clearly if he was down here, she hadn't woken him up and he'd been awake already.

"Can't sleep?" he asked.

She shook her head. "I thought I'd get a snack."

"There's leftover pizza in the fridge," he offered.

Cassie nodded. "That was my plan." She walked to the other room, looking back over her shoulder at him. He'd sat back down again. Was it too soon to clear the air and try to talk about why she'd left?

Not that she planned to explain why. She didn't understand herself well enough to attempt that. But she could at least apologize…

She took a deep breath, tried to work up her nerve. Maybe she'd talk now, before she got her snack. "Hey, Jake?"

"Shh." He cut her off, but from the look on his face, it wasn't because he didn't want to hear what she had to say. It was because he'd heard something and he was on alert—his shoulders were tensed. He had been sitting with his back against the back of the chair but now he was leaning forward.

"What?" Cassie whispered, but Jake was already up, moving to one of the front windows. Instinctively she stepped back against the wall, into a darkened corner.

He walked from the first window to the second.

This time she heard the noise too, but it sounded like it was coming from the back of the house, not the front where Jake was.

"Jake," she whispered as loud as she dared, motioning with her head behind her.

"Get upstairs. Hide."

His tone left no room for argument as he moved toward the back door and Cassie hurried to the stairs, keeping her back against the wall. He hadn't needed to tell her to go up there. Her son, *their* son, was in that room and nothing would stop Cassie from doing her best to protect him.

As she rushed up the stairs, she tried to pinpoint where she'd heard the noise but all was quiet.

She opened the door of the large closet in the bedroom, pulled Will from the bed and settled him in the corner of it. He slept harder than anyone she knew, something for which she was extremely thankful right now. Then she pulled the door shut behind her.

Please don't let him find me. Another prayer. She didn't have time to analyze why praying seemed so natural here. She felt less alone somehow, which was interesting since she wasn't even sure what she believed about God.

Cassie tried to be as quiet as possible, but it seemed

like every time she shifted it was the loudest sound she'd ever heard. She tried not to move so much, made an effort to even slow her breathing down enough that it wouldn't make so much noise either.

She heard a door open, the creaking loud like one of the main heavy doors downstairs to the outside. Relief flooded her and she almost called out to let Jake know where she was. Hadn't he gone outside? So it would make sense if he had that he'd come back in once he'd checked things out and determined everything was okay.

At the last second though, she stopped herself. It could just as easily be whoever was after her. She knew that. So instead she didn't move, didn't make a sound.

Whoever had come inside didn't speak either. Did that mean the chances were more likely that it wasn't Jake? She swallowed hard and hoped her logic was faulty, but somehow she didn't think it was.

There were footsteps, then a creaking noise, followed by another creaking noise. The stairs? Was he coming up to her room? Her heartbeat, already going faster than she was comfortable with, pounding in her throat in a way that made swallowing difficult, sped up even more. Cassie swallowed hard. Waited.

There was silence for a period of time, and she tried to guess how many minutes had passed, in case it mattered later. Two? Three? He hadn't been upstairs long by the time she heard creaking again that seemed to indicate he was going back down the stairs. But he'd been up there longer than was necessary just to look inside her room and see that she wasn't in it. Had he been taking the time to search for her? Or was he setting up some kind of trap in the room where she was supposed to be safe?

Her current line of thinking made Cassie shudder.

She wasn't much of a risk taker these days. The amount of risk now being asked of her... It was a lot to take in. More than she wanted to handle.

The stairs creaked again. Wait, was he coming back up? The footsteps grew louder and came closer. Cassie felt her heartbeat skip.

Another door opened.

"Hey!" That was Jake yelling now.

The footsteps moved faster, back down the stairs? Cassie heard the pace quicken like whoever had come inside first was running. Then the front door opened. She heard more running and imagined Jake chasing him, which was her best guess as to what was going on right now. Fear for his life enveloped her. What if he was killed keeping her safe? She wouldn't be able to live with that knowledge.

Easing forward out of her crouched position, she reached for the door and pushed it open again, then stood, looking for something on the shelf to use as a weapon. All she saw were cans of vegetables in doomsday-prepper sizes. It wasn't unusual for Alaskans to keep emergency food and water stored in closets, in case of earthquakes or other natural disasters that could cut Alaska off from the road system or the port. She grabbed a Costco-sized can of green beans from the shelf. It wasn't much as far as weaponry was concerned, but it was better than the nothing she currently had.

The bedroom was empty, still dark. Did she dare leave Will? She decided the answer to that was no, but crept closer toward the door, where she could lean out of it and see down the stairs and into the living room. From her vantage point, she saw that the door was open.

For the first time, Cassie remembered her phone was

in her pocket and called 911 to report that they'd had an intruder. She wasn't able to give more details, but they said they'd come right over.

She started to move back into the bedroom, then movement caught her eye. She raised the green beans.

"What are you doing?" Jake stood in the doorway. He was out of breath, but it didn't quell the emotions in his voice. He cared about keeping her safe. Sure, she'd known he was a good guy and always, *always* did the right thing. But something in his tone just now made her wonder if…

No, he couldn't still care about her beyond how he'd feel about anyone in danger. She shouldn't even let her mind go there.

"Didn't I tell you to hide?" he continued.

She cleared her throat. "I heard noises." It was a lame excuse when she said it aloud. "Did you see him?"

Jake shook his head. "I went outside to check and didn't see anything, but when I came inside I thought I heard something. I yelled and then heard him run down the stairs. He must have come in when I stepped outside, like he was watching me for a chance to come in." He shook his head again. "Beyond stupid of me. I should have stayed inside. Anyway, I stood for half a second longer than I should have, trying to decide if I should come up and check on the two of you or chase him. By the time I decided catching him was top priority, I couldn't catch up." Jake's features were colored with emotion. "He had a car waiting just down the road and he had too much of a head start."

"What kind of car?" Cassie asked, not that she knew what anyone around town was driving these days, so the answer really wouldn't tell her anything.

"A black SUV—a Toyota, I think. It was too dark to be sure."

Just as she'd thought, the information was meaningless to her since she didn't know anyone's cars anymore.

The last thing she wanted to be was a damsel in distress who needed help, but tonight she was at a loss and she didn't like the feeling. "I called the police," she offered as her one contribution.

"The police may want to talk to you again." Jake shook his head. "I'm not sure. Maybe they'll just be able to see if he left any evidence."

She felt self-conscious enough around Jake in her pajamas, though they were a long-sleeved shirt and pants that one of the women on Jake's team had left for her. Her suitcase of belongings she'd brought to Alaska was still in her car, abandoned when she was being tailed. Cassie had to remember to get the car tomorrow. Will would need a change of clothes also, although for tonight he'd been delighted at the idea of sleeping in his blue jeans.

"I think I'll change." She didn't have a bathrobe or anything like that, so switching back into jeans seemed like her best option.

"I'll wait in the hall." Jake folded his arms and leaned back against the wall across from her bedroom door before she could argue. Having him close made her feel stronger, although she wasn't sure she wanted to admit it. When he was here, she felt as though she were on solid ground, could make more confident decisions. Even though she'd been reminded of her mortality multiple times today, being near Jake made her feel she could stop and think while she decided how to work this problem.

She liked this feeling too much. Always had. It wasn't

safe to depend on a person that way, was it? To know you were better because of them, to be used to having that person in your day…

Because she'd learned the day her mom disappeared that people weren't always dependable, they left.

It was entirely possible, if she tried to emotionally dissect the past, that it had been part of the problem with Jake—the fact that there weren't problems. He was her better half, the one man she wanted to be by her side forever. She'd always been able to count on him, and that scared her. Shouldn't she have learned from her mother's abandonment not to count on anyone?

Had she invented the problems she'd worried about to give her an excuse to leave? The fact that they'd both wanted to be doctors, that she'd wanted to make her own way in the world. Was it really just as simple as her having a fear of being left, of getting hurt again?

Cassie sighed deeply, letting her shoulders fall. Analyzing it wouldn't do a bit of good. Nothing she could do would allow her to go back and change the past. Puzzling out their history together just confused her when she needed a clear head now more than ever.

So she pulled her clothes back on, resolved that she was going to do the best she could to help solve this case and get back out of Jake's life. As much as she'd messed it up the first time around, she owed him that much.

Now to figure out how she could help when she hadn't the slightest clue how to search for missing persons or how to hunt down attackers.

The rest of the night passed without incident. Jake knew, because he sat outside Cassie and Will's door as the dusky summer shadows darkened and then lightened again almost in the blink of an eye. He sat there, wondering if she was sleeping, trying to sort out how they were going to handle this situation.

Her attackers meant business, Jake didn't doubt that at all. He stood and stretched, moving toward the stairs to make some coffee, now that it was fully light and a time of day where people were up and attackers would be less likely to strike. Whoever was after her was fairly coordinated, had a plan. Their execution had failed, for which Jake was thankful, but the hard truth was that he'd been unprepared last night. He wouldn't let that happen again.

Movement behind him as he reached for the coffee carafe to fill it with water startled him and he whipped his head around, arms coming up in a defensive stance.

"Easy there, killer." Cassie's face almost cracked a smile. She looked tired, dark circles growing under her eyes. That answered that question. He was almost certain she hadn't slept at all.

"Not funny, given last night."

Her face sobered. "You're right. I wanted to talk to you about that."

"Last night?" He held his breath, waiting to hear if she wanted to talk about the people after her or their son. He needed to discuss Will, but he didn't know if he was ready to face the hurt that conversation would bring. In an odd way, it was easier to talk about the people who were out to get her, or her missing aunt.

Jake busied his hands making the coffee, finding it hard to see her standing there, all vulnerable and beautiful and so close to him he had to catch his breath.

"I want to help."

He breathed out. He'd been prepped for it. Cassie wasn't a woman to sit on the sidelines.

"It's going to be dangerous, you know," he started, noting the way her eyebrows went up in immediate reaction to his words. He raised his hands in mock surrender. "Hey, I'm making sure you understand."

"Is there anything about my life right now that doesn't strike you as dangerous?"

Something had changed in her since last night. Her fire, one of the things he'd loved about her way back when, had returned with an extra spark. Yesterday she'd seemed defeated. Tired. Today she was ready to fight, and it seemed to bode well.

He was confident in his team, but having her along would help them too. She knew her aunt, knew the areas she was likely to frequent, could tell them about how she would have thought and made decisions if she was on her own or hiking somewhere against her will. With the new information they'd learned about the disappearance likely being intentional and relating to foul play, they'd change how they searched, shift their parameters. Raven Pass Search and Rescue was good at what they did. They'd find Cassie's aunt. Jake wasn't naive enough to be sure she'd be alive when they got there though, something he wasn't sure if Cassie had considered.

"What?" Her facial expression wavered, and he wished he knew her as well as he used to. If he did, he might be able to tell what she was thinking. She was being so brave, handling what yesterday had thrown at her with spunk and grace.

Without thinking, he brushed back a piece of hair from her face. Her eyes widened and she blinked in that way only a woman can, not seeming to know how attractive and innocent she looked.

"Jake…" Her voice trailed off as the impact of years of missing her and of the danger in her life suddenly threatened to overwhelm him, and he stepped closer to her. She lifted her chin, only millimeters, but enough that it almost read like an invitation.

He bent closer, his eyes on her lips.

Stopped.

Their eyes met, and if hers had been unreadable before, he felt like now was the opposite. Her eyes were like clear pools, full of open honesty. He suspected the same could be said of his.

The truth he saw in her eyes, knew was reflected in his own, was this: neither of them was over each other.

But that didn't make rekindling something a good idea. It was still a terrible one. He'd learned his lesson the first time she'd broken his heart, thank you.

He pulled away, turned to the coffee maker and pushed a button to start the brew cycle, then turned around to face her. "Your aunt may not be alive when we find her."

"I know that. Why tell me something fairly obvious?"

"I wanted to make sure you'd considered that before you offered to help." Jake shoved a hand through his hair, shaking his head. And break whatever craziness had come over them that had almost had them kissing in his kitchen a day after he saw her again for the first time in seven years.

"Listen, Jake, I think things through now, okay? I have to."

"Then yes, we'd like your help." He tried to sound as professional as he could, though admittedly he'd probably lost any measure of professional distance earlier when he'd had to fight the urge to kiss her.

But it hadn't just been him, had it? He'd seen it in her eyes too, in the tilt of her chin.

Still didn't make it a good idea. He should have learned from having her hurt him the first time.

He tried again. "Truly, Cassie. It would help a lot to have you there."

The defensiveness in her posture seemed to ease some. Her shoulders untensed. "Thank you."

He nodded.

"I'm going to go get ready. I'm guessing we'll leave soon, right? I don't want to sit around drinking coffee while my aunt is out there, in who knows what kind of shape."

"I've got travel mugs for the coffee. We can go as soon as you're ready."

She hurried up the stairs and Jake went to his own room to shower and change, praying as he did that God would be with their search today. Not only for them to find Cassie's aunt, but for God to keep them safe.

Physically.

And their hearts.

For a minute this morning, Cassie had thought he was going to kiss her.

Then just as quickly as the moment had begun, it was over and Jake was even more reserved than he'd been the day before. Cassie had avoided being alone with him for the rest of the morning, relieved beyond words when Will woke up, and even more relieved when it was time to go meet Jake's team for the day's work.

They'd pulled into her aunt's driveway and Cassie

fought regret at the years she'd spent away from home. What if she didn't see her aunt again? She could never go back and give them more time together, and the thought overwhelmed her.

"We'll do the best we can, okay?" Jake squeezed her hand, let go as quickly as he'd grabbed it.

But it was something, a show of kindness in a day that Cassie could already feel was going to be difficult, and she appreciated that.

She hadn't explained much to Will, who was going with them. Jake had talked to a friend at the police department who agreed that it was safest for him to be with his mom, but that location didn't matter right now. They seemed to be in some degree of danger, no matter where they were, as the intrusion in the house last night had proven. Will knew Cassie's aunt was missing, but she'd been vague about today's events, mostly framing it as a hike they were going on.

He was interested, knowing she'd lived here before. Why hadn't she realized how curious he was about her past?

It further reinforced the need to tell him more of his own history. Like who his father was. She'd spoken of Jake to Will. She hadn't wanted her son to think he didn't have a dad, or wonder too much. So she'd told him stories—the good ones—and about what a good man his father was. Because it was true. Her leaving had never had anything to do with Jake's character. At least not his flaws.

No, Jake had always been perfect. Maybe sometimes too perfect for someone like her to feel like she measured up.

"You're sure you know where you're going up here? It's been a long time," Jake said.

"I'll manage fine." She moved away from him, turned her attention to making sure Will was ready, that his shoes were tied tight enough and that she herself was able to maintain some level of composure. Jake's questions echoed her own. Was she sure that she would be able to help? Cassie didn't even have an answer for herself. But she knew these trails, she knew her aunt, and she had to try.

Most of Jake's team arrived in an old red Jeep. Piper, who was driving, parked it and she, Ellie and Caleb piled out. They were missing one. *Adriana*, Cassie thought.

"Where's Adriana?" Jake asked, confirming that Cassie had indeed remembered the absent member's name correctly.

"She rode with the police. They are meeting us here because they want to come too."

"They're letting her dog ride in the police car?"

Piper shook her head, and then Cassie noticed a leash and a dog jumped out. Some kind of Lab mix, maybe. "Babe rode with us."

"Babe?" Cassie raised her eyebrows, unable to reconcile the serious woman she'd met with a dog named Babe.

"As in Babe Ruth. Adriana's a huge baseball fan, especially the Yankees," Ellie explained.

A police cruiser pulled up before Cassie had the chance to respond, which was probably good because she knew very little about baseball and even less about the Yankees. Will had asked to play T-ball last year for the first time and Cassie had almost signed him up but had to back out at the last minute because she couldn't work it around her job and daycare schedule for him. Yet another thing he was missing out on because he didn't have a dad. Or, well, he did but not in his life.

Another failing that was hers alone to own.

She looked back at the police car. The driver's side door opened, and Officer Wicks, who Cassie had met the day before, stepped out. Adriana climbed out of the passenger side and immediately went to her dog and started petting him like they'd been separated for days instead of maybe half an hour at most, Cassie guessed.

"Everyone ready?" Jake asked the group as a whole, then directed his attention to Officer Wicks. "Officer Wicks, you ready?"

The man appeared to have given up on Jake using his first name when they were working, because he didn't make nearly as much of a face as he had the night before.

"I'm ready when the rest of you are," Officer Wicks answered. "Thanks for letting me join you. I don't intend to interrupt your usual search procedures. I just want to be on hand in case we find…any evidence of a crime scene."

His eyes darted toward Cassie and she heard the unspoken message, gripped Will's hand a little tighter though she hadn't meant to. Jake didn't expect to find her aunt alive.

But Cassie had to believe. Had to try anyway.

Officer Wicks continued. "I also want to be on hand to observe some of the…unorthodox methods your team uses to search, to assure the department and anyone involved in a trial later that you were supervised."

Cassie thought she saw Adriana bristle from where she stood beside her dog. Was that what he meant, he wanted to supervise the use of the dog? She sure seemed to have taken something personally. Or maybe she was one of those people whose facial expressions didn't always display what they were actually feeling.

Officer Wicks looked in Adriana's direction, and to Cassie it almost looked like he wanted to say something to her and then shook his head slightly. Interesting. The vibe between them intrigued Cassie's secret romantic side and she wondered if anything was going on between them, or if it was just tension she was misreading.

"Anyway, I'm ready." Officer Wicks looked back at Jake.

"Okay. Cassie is going to take us on some of the trails her aunt used to use. Follow her. This area overlaps our previous search area to a degree, from what she told me, but then branches off into an area where we didn't go. She sketched out a map for me and I emailed each of you a copy in case we get separated for any reason, or we need to split into groups. Be aware, some of it's pretty overgrown."

"That's good news for me," Adriana mumbled as they all started walking and she came into the line just behind Cassie. Cassie guessed she was in the front because she was leading, and then Adriana was next because of the dog. Cassie was enough of an animal person to think it was cool that the dog could help in some way.

Will looked over at the dog and, reading his mind the way moms do, Cassie reminded him not to pet it and told him that the dog was working.

Cassie looked over at Adriana after walking in silence for a minute, too intrigued by her work with the dog to resist asking the question. "What did you mean earlier about it being good news for you?"

Adriana motioned around them. "In an area like

this, the scent disperses quickly and mingles with other scents. The integrity is degraded a lot sooner. In an area like Jake is describing, with thick brush, the scent could get trapped and will linger much longer, making it easier for Babe to identify the scent he's looking for."

"So he's a search-and-rescue dog?"

"Yes."

Though she was trying to keep her hope from rising too high for fear of the crash that would come with disappointment, Cassie felt her expectations lifting anyway. The idea that the dog was trained to do something humans couldn't fully understand intrigued her.

"Mind if I join y'all up here in front?" Jake's voice was barely winded despite the fact that Cassie was keeping a pace that had her catching her breath frequently. Will was up for the challenge—he was the very definition of an active boy—and Cassie knew she shouldn't have been surprised to see Jake not breaking a sweat, face completely relaxed and not betraying any effort whatsoever.

She was also surprised anew by how good-looking he was. He'd been handsome before. But this new fully grown man version of Jake was even more attractive, so much so she was startled whenever she glanced at him.

"Sure, if it's fine with Cassie." Adriana looked at her and Cassie found herself wanting to tell the woman the whole story. Right now no one but her and Jake knew the truth about Will and it was weighing on Cassie. She needed a friend. Maybe Adriana wouldn't mind being one? She was certainly perceptive enough, in a way Cassie couldn't quantify. Much like the way the dog had skills no one could quite pinpoint, Adriana seemed like the kind of woman who saw things others couldn't.

Cassie was certainly under the impression that Adriana knew there was more to Cassie and Jake's relationship than old friends.

"It's fine." Such a multi-purpose word, *fine*. Able to mean everything from *yes, this is great, I don't mind at all* to *actually it's not fine with me at all but sure*.

Her current use of *fine* was leaning more to the second.

"Great." Jake smiled at her, still looking wary, like he was scared to get close to her, even while they were hiking. But the weird vibe from this morning, after the "almost kiss," was gone.

She braced herself for conversation with him, but he looked down instead, started talking to Will.

"So how's it going with you today, little man?"

"I'm not a little man. I'm just a kid. I'm six." Will picked up a stick from the side of the trail. "See this? It's my gun in case we see any bad guys."

She resisted a comment about bringing a stick to a gunfight, but still felt herself crack a slight smile. With any luck, there wouldn't be any bad guys today. Really, she didn't even think they needed luck. It was broad daylight and they were a large group. She didn't feel any of the foreboding that she had last night, and while she knew she needed to keep her guard up, she felt confident that today was, at least, a chance to breathe.

"Have you been on hikes like this before?" Jake was asking Will. Talking to his son and not telling him who he really was. Cassie needed to have a conversation with Will, explain the truth to him as soon as possible.

"No, we don't hike in Florida. Mom just goes to work and I go to school, and then we go home."

Jake's eyes swung to Cassie's. His eyebrows were

raised and she heard all of his questions. Yes, she'd once been a more active, adventurous person. Yes, time had changed her. A lot.

"Well, I'm glad you're getting to hike here. I loved hiking when I was a kid."

"I like it so far. Especially because Mom said when you hike, you get snacks. She packed marshmallows for me."

"That's great, bud!"

"My name is Will."

"Not so much into nicknames, are you?"

"Not when they're not my name. But I do like marshmallows. Did you pack any?"

Jake laughed, his face looking more relaxed than Cassie had seen it in years. All of this, the entire interaction between him and their son was too much for her heart to handle. She smiled a little, ignoring the stabbing in her chest, and then focused her attention on the trail, letting Will lag behind her slightly. "You'll stay with him?" She double-checked with Jake.

He met her eyes and nodded.

She pushed her pace harder, letting the burning in her legs and lungs drown out the pain in her heart.

And letting all of it push from her mind the idea that she was being stalked by someone who wanted to bring her pain.

FOUR

Jake had always considered himself a multitasker. So he was able to talk to his son—still wrapping his mind around that one—and keep half an eye on Cassie up ahead, all the while not letting himself forget that there could be trouble on this hike, more than Levi Wicks would be prepared to handle on his own even though he was an excellent officer.

He was fairly confident they should be okay or he wouldn't have let Cassie bring Will. Exposing Will to danger wouldn't be okay for any reason. But Jake couldn't control this environment as well as he could many others and that fact was making him nervous.

The woods were quiet today, still. Some days the wind blew hard and made it almost impossible to hear the person next to you, but today was the opposite and the hush was getting to him, making him antsy deep down.

"So did you sleep okay last night?" he asked Will, wondering if he knew anything about the events of the night before.

"Yeah, I slept fine. I usually do." He shrugged, used his stick to whack some fireweed growing beside the trail. "Can we stop talking now? I'm getting tired."

The kid said what he was thinking, that was for sure. Something he'd gotten from Jake or Cassie? He'd have said Cassie because she'd never been the type of person to hide how she felt. But he wasn't sure anymore. Who could be engaged to someone, seem like everything was going fine, and then just disappear with no explanation? Come back seven years later with a kid?

Hurt made him want to say he'd never really known her at all, a bitter thought. But he knew none of that was true and wouldn't be helpful anyway. He'd known her well. She'd just reacted out of fear. Or maybe she'd changed her mind about him. Either way, Jake didn't believe her to be capable of deceit.

They still needed to hash this out, and he wanted the full story. Not just about Will but on why she'd left. Her aunt's disappearance and her own jeopardy were getting in the way of that conversation. Maybe that wasn't a bad thing. Maybe God was giving him time to accept the news of his paternity before he delved into the reasons Cassie had hidden it from him, let alone left him.

He hiked along without talking anymore, but he kept watching Will. The kid pressed on with admirable determination. It didn't sound like this was the kind of thing he was used to, but he was doing a good job. It was hard to picture a son of his being raised away from these mountains that surrounded Raven Pass, but Will fit right in here.

Was Cassie planning to just leave when the search was over? And what, have Will fly up in the summers to visit him? He didn't want to be a summer-vacation dad. He wanted to be a real one, starting today.

God, help me because I'm not even sure I know how.
His dad was amazing, so it wasn't that Jake lacked for

inspiration. He just wasn't sure how to put it into play in his own life. A son was obviously top priority over things like work. But he still had a job and needed to do it well. How would that all fit together?

One day at a time.

He took a deep breath, looked around them. Cassie was still ahead with Adriana, and Babe was sniffing, working the area like he'd seen the dog do so many times before. He'd been skeptical at one point at the idea of trusting an animal as a full-on teammate, but Babe had proven it was worth it. More than, really. He looked behind him. Piper and Caleb were deep in conversation but their eyes scanned back and forth over the terrain, looking for any aberrations in the landscape that could indicate a struggle, or someone taking the wrong path. Ellie and Levi brought up the rear.

Help us find her, God.

"What are your thoughts on this?" Levi's voice asked him only a few minutes later. He must have hiked up ahead of Piper and Caleb.

"On Mabel's disappearance?"

Levi nodded.

"It seemed reasonable to believe it was an accident until Cassie showed up and things started happening. At this point…" Jake trailed off. No need to voice what he was thinking, but Levi seemed to understand. Their chances of finding the woman alive were slim.

Jake had seen Cassie's eyes, knew the hope there that she'd tried to temper. He hoped she could bear up under the storm he feared was coming.

"I agree." Levi nodded and Jake turned to his friend, confused about why Levi had been so ready to accept

Cassie's help to show them Mabel's preferred hiking routes.

"So why these trails? This is where she hiked, but you don't think she disappeared while hiking."

"I didn't say that." Levi said the words slowly. "I don't think she disappeared of her own volition. Or even by accident. But that doesn't mean it wasn't around here. According to Cassie, her aunt hiked every day and told her niece about these trails often. Someone watching her would know her routine, and be aware of the best places to attack."

"What you're saying makes sense, just not for Raven Pass." Jake shook his head. "The man showing up last night was strange enough for this town, but you're saying it may not even have been a crime of opportunity. That someone might actually have targeted an older woman and done some kind of harm to her?"

Levi didn't answer right away. Jake respected the fact that as law enforcement, his friend had lines he couldn't cross, things he couldn't share with him. But he knew from that look that Levi had reason to believe his assumptions were correct. He hadn't found the body, or he would have told Jake and he wouldn't have them all out there.

What did he know then that they didn't?

"We found forensic evidence at the house."

"You know who it was?"

"No." Levi shook his head. "Unless someone has committed a crime, or has some other kind of exception that would make their fingerprints stay in the system, their prints may not be available to match immediately."

"But there are prints."

Levi nodded.

"She had friends though. Surely that explains it."

"Mabel had a .44, like any good Alaskan."

Quite the non sequitur, but okay. Jake nodded.

"There are prints on the safe that match the prints on the door and around the house in other places."

Jake didn't want to consider his next question, or the ones that followed. "And the weapon?"

"Missing."

The farther she hiked, the more the past came back to chase Cassie. Every step through the alders as the trail twisted deeper into the woods and the brushy foliage that gave way to tall spruce trees and thick vegetation seemed to bring her closer to who she had been. Seven years ago.

Her aunt's disappearance hurt even more now that she was back on these familiar trails, battling with what had been and what was true now. The rift between herself and Jake wasn't something Cassie could fix. She knew that. A person made choices in life, but she didn't always get to go back and change them. Still, she wished she could tell her aunt about the situation, get her thoughts on how to handle it.

Why did everyone she love leave her?

Something inside corrected the thought as soon as it appeared. Jake hadn't left her. She took another step, looked at the way the trail was disappearing and tried to remember if they went left or right here.

"I'm hungry, Mom."

Will had caught up to her again. Cassie slowed her pace as she bent to talk to him. "Sorry, bud. I have snacks, but it's not quite time to stop, okay? About another half mile." If she remembered correctly, they'd come to a turnaround point up there. They could stop for snacks and then Jake or Officer Wicks, or whoever was in charge, could decide if they wanted her to keep going.

The truth was that Cassie didn't think it was likely her aunt would have hiked in even this far. She had years ago, but she'd gotten older, and surely that would have slowed her down some. Besides that, she just didn't feel they needed to go any farther. How much did intuition play into situations like this? Cassie wasn't sure.

"You okay?"

Now Jake's voice. She really needed to up her situational awareness for people coming up behind her apparently.

"I'm fine," she answered without thinking, sighed and tried again. "I'm tired. Tired of not knowing if she's okay, not sure if I should let the search go for today... She isn't here, I don't think."

Jake nodded, not commenting. He'd always been good at listening.

"I just..." She trailed off.

"I know."

And she believed in the moment that he did. He knew her fear of what they would eventually find.

They stopped for a snack at a place where the trail widened into a meadow, which had fireweed just starting to bloom around the edges. The sky was bright blue above them and for a few minutes Cassie felt her shoulders relax. Like she could breathe here. But their rest didn't last long.

"We need to leave." Officer Wicks's voice was steel, his expression all-business.

Jake nodded immediately, started shoving Will's pile

of snacks and trash into his own backpack. "All right, let's go."

Will nodded, childlike trust on his face.

Cassie felt none of that trust. She had questions.

"Now."

Officer Wicks's directive left no time for her to get answers.

They were back on the trail, hiking at a faster pace this time. Officer Wicks was ahead of the group now, and it wasn't lost on Cassie that his eyes never stopped scanning the path ahead. His hand was at his side, presumably on his weapon.

What had changed? What was going on? Surely someone should tell her, the actual potential victim, right?

She wanted to ask Jake, who was at her side, matching his pace to hers perfectly, which she suspected was intentional. But she didn't want Will to hear the answer.

Did she need to know?

Cassie exhaled, pushed her pace faster and tried to focus her mind anywhere it would land. The gorgeous desolation of deep woods like this. The pace of Babe, Adriana's dog, up ahead of her. According to Adriana, whom she'd talked to while they were taking their snack break, the dog hadn't alerted to Cassie's aunt's scent at all. Which didn't mean she *hadn't* come this way, Adriana had said, trying to leave her a scrap of hope.

Hoping was starting to hurt Cassie more than it helped. No one told you that there was a blackness underneath hope that was nothing more than positive thinking. Was that why Jake put his hope in something more, in trusting God instead of just thinking and wishing for the best?

The foliage started to change again, grew less thick,

the trees less tall. They were close to where they were parked. Half a mile? Give or take?

The first gunshot hit the dust at Cassie's feet, the noise exploding in a sudden sharp snap of sound.

"Will, get down!" she yelled when she knew what it was, tackling her son and rolling into the cover of the alders.

"Was that a gun, Mommy?"

She'd never thought she'd have to answer that question. Her heart pounded, thudding a terrified rhythm in her ears and then there was a weight on top of her. She tensed, almost fought it off and then realized it was Jake. He'd dove on top of her to shelter her the way she had her son.

Without a second thought. Ready to sacrifice his own life.

Cassie wanted time alone to think, figure out what this meant, if anything, but processing time was a luxury people didn't have when there was a gunman in the woods and they were pinned down under bushes with no means of escape.

Another gunshot. Then another. Who were they shooting at? Cassie would have assumed it was at her, but none of the shots were hitting very close, so maybe she wasn't the target after all. Who then? Jake? The people around her?

"What do we do?" Cassie whispered to Jake. The branches were too thick to crawl through, it seemed to her. But wasn't a moving target better than one lying still? Then again, moving could expose Will and she wouldn't let him be hurt.

She never should have let him come today. Why had

she assumed the daylight would ensure their safety? Maybe because coming after them didn't make sense.

Unless they had come close to finding something.

Another flicker of hope, even as the shots stopped and the stillness returned to the woods.

Will started to cry. Cassie's already broken heart broke again.

"You're okay, buddy."

Jake's voice was solid, powerful but calming, soothing in a way that washed over her like a swift glacial river.

"Everyone all right?" Officer Wicks's voice.

No, Cassie wanted to say. She wasn't all right. None of them were.

God, why?

She'd wondered earlier if Jake trusted God because it was a more solid base for his hopes than positive thinking. But was it really? Couldn't the God of the universe have stopped the shots in the first place, rather than just protecting them through it? For that matter, why had He let her aunt disappear if He was really in charge and could change things like that?

Jake's faith hadn't been something that divided them years ago, even though they'd disagreed on issues. Like whether or not "waiting" for marriage was fully necessary.

But now Cassie felt further from him, even though his body was just above hers, pressed against her back like a shield.

How could he believe in a God who cared but let bad things happen?

"We're okay over here," Jake answered for all three of them.

Physically, Cassie supposed, it was true.

"Why didn't you shoot back at them?" she asked the officer when she saw that his weapon was drawn.

"I never had a clear shot. I saw muzzle flash that way." He gestured to a rise in the land that Cassie could see would have made a good place for a shooter to hide. "But you should never shoot at an unknown target."

Cop shows didn't always get it right, Cassie realized. She opened her mouth to apologize for questioning his judgment, but he was already on his phone, calling the incident in and asking for officers to canvas that hillside and see if any evidence was left behind.

Jake climbed off her and Cassie let Will move away from her. He wiped another stray tear from his face, but besides that, he'd stopped crying quickly. Kids were resilient, people said. She was extremely thankful that appeared to be true.

But kids weren't invincible. And while Cassie had never dreamed she was really allowing Will to be in danger today, she was certainly not going to put him at risk again. If that meant she had to lock them both up inside some kind of safe house, she wouldn't fight it. Whatever it took to keep him safe.

Running appealed to her, straight back to Florida. But she knew their safety there would only be an illusion.

"I'm hit." Ellie's voice wasn't very close, and Cassie had to look around to find her. She was ten, fifteen feet away. She must have been behind them on the trail.

"How bad?" Jake had started moving that way as soon as she'd spoken up. Now he bent over, looked at the site.

"Not badly. Just a graze on the outside of my left arm."

Not far enough away from her heart to make any

of them breathe deeply. If the shot had been six, eight inches to the right...

Cassie pulled Will close to her, running her hand through his hair. To reassure him or herself, she wasn't sure.

"You okay, bud?"

"I'll feel better when we are back inside." His little voice was honest, a quiver in it. Cassie squeezed him tighter, then looked to Jake, who was looking over at her.

"Let me help Ellie. I'm a nurse," Cassie said.

"No. You need to stay down. I'll take care of it."

Jake held her gaze for a minute, but a look she once would have been able to read was perplexing to her now, so much time had come between them. Finally he glanced away, swung his backpack down off of his shoulders and rummaged through it. For a first aid kit, she was guessing.

Cassie scanned the area around them, fought against full-body shakes, only somewhat successfully. It wasn't safe to just stop here. It couldn't be.

"We need to move," Officer Wicks spoke up. "Jake, do what you can quickly and we'll take better care of it when we get to town. Sorry, Ellie." He shrugged but she nodded, understanding their situation.

They started hiking again, faster this time, and Cassie kept her eyes roving, looking for a threat she knew was out there somewhere.

Someone had shot at them today, and could still be watching even now. She had a son to keep safe, to keep raising. She couldn't afford to be an easy target for the shooter.

And yet any moment she could be.

Cassie walked faster.

FIVE

No way was Jake letting his son walk into something like that again. The determination beat against his chest, in rhythm with his heartbeat, as he hiked down the trail, conscious of the weight of responsibility pressing on him. He was the leader of the team, should be the protector of his son, and they'd walked straight into some kind of trap.

Not a trap, because no one had told them to go there. They hadn't received any anonymous tips. They'd investigated the area because Cassie had suggested it. Surely it didn't mean she was in league with whoever had her aunt?

Jake glanced back at her, dismissed the idea immediately. It was a coincidence he was uncomfortable with, but it was explained away in many more logical ways than Cassie having changed so drastically, or having put her son in danger. More likely, one of the cars was being tracked or one of the phones was tapped. Or, even more possible because it was easier to pull off, someone was watching them.

"I'm going to go ahead and check out the cars and

make sure nothing has been sabotaged." Levi motioned down the trail. "Can you handle things from here?"

"Yes."

"Jake, I don't think we're going to find her aunt, at least not alive. I need Cassie to stay alive."

So did Jake. Just not for the same reasons. He nodded though. "I have a .44 in case of bears."

"And other threats?" Levi seemed to be taking his measure, weighing whether or not Jake was willing to protect Cassie no matter what. Jake squared his shoulders, did his best to communicate his answer.

Levi nodded. "Thanks."

It was a job Jake would have done anyway—he didn't need to be asked or thanked, but he nodded back and watched his friend hurry down the trail.

Jake looked back at the group with him. Piper and Caleb were walking in front and in back of Cassie and Will, respectively. His team was already helping him. Adriana was right behind Jake, Ellie behind her. He noticed she was keeping a good pace, so her wound wasn't slowing her down.

"Are you okay, Boss?" Adriana asked him. He smiled at her teasing nickname. He was the leader of the group, but he wasn't anyone's boss, not really. A team leader wasn't the same thing.

"I'm not the one someone's trying to kill," Jake muttered, the words making the situation even more real. He turned right when the trail came to a fork, glanced back to make sure everyone followed him. When he did so, he noticed the look on Adriana's face, her eyebrows raised, expression questioning.

"I know." Her words were quiet.

Did all of his team suspect that he still had feelings

for Cassie? Or just Adriana? The woman reminded him of her dog sometimes, able to understand things, sense what most people couldn't.

It was eerie. Extremely helpful during searching. And just as annoying when it came to his personal life.

Then again, having someone else know...

He nodded. "Thanks for asking. I'm as okay as I can be." He considered his words carefully, not wanting to share too much with a team member.

She smiled. "She's a pretty cool woman. Tough. She's the one people talk about, isn't she?"

"What?" Jake didn't have to feign surprise. He had no idea what she was talking about.

He turned ahead, scanned the terrain before them. No threats that he could see, though the unseen ones were even scarier, always looming there unable to be neutralized.

"When they're talking about why you don't date..." Adriana trailed off. "Okay, you really don't know what I'm talking about. I'm sorry, Jake. It's really not appropriate of me to pass on gossip anyway. I shouldn't have said anything."

"Don't worry about it."

His shoulders relaxed, relieved to have that conversation over. But the effects still lingered. People talked about him? Jake supposed he shouldn't be surprised. Raven Pass was a small town, full of Alaskan moms who would be happy with their single daughters marrying a paramedic who always planned to stay in town. He'd taken to turning down dates, so it followed reason that people must speculate about why. And it wouldn't be hard. He'd dated a little, about a year or so after Cassie had left. But he'd never made it past one date with anyone, and finally the last woman he'd been out with he'd had to apologize to and tell her he couldn't date because he was still in love with his former fiancée.

So yeah, they probably talked.

The parking lot finally came into view up ahead and Jake exhaled. They'd made it this far. He could see Levi and another officer bent over cars, looking underneath and at engines.

"What's the verdict?" Jake asked as they approached.

Levi shook his head. "No tracking devices, so that's not how he found us."

Of course, that would have been too easy. Find the tracking device, get rid of it, problem solved. However else the shooter was doing his surveillance was going to be much more difficult to mitigate.

"Do you need us around here?" Jake asked as the others caught up to him. He stole a glance at Cassie. She was still holding Will tightly to her side, but she looked more composed than earlier, even if her shoulders were still so tight they practically came up to her ears.

"No."

"Good. I'd rather get her inside."

"What about the rest of your team?" Levi asked, eyes on Adriana and her dog. "Are they finished searching for the day?"

Jake didn't speak up at first. He gave them all a second to think, then turned to his team. "I'm going with Cassie today and am going to figure out something better for security than hoping the bad guys miss."

Cassie opened her mouth to argue. Yes, he knew she wanted her aunt found. But he was starting to think Levi was right. This was no longer a rescue mission—it was a recovery. Living people, potential victims, took priority. And for Jake, Cassie and Will took priority over any aspect of this case. He shook his head and she closed her mouth.

"We're going back out, on one of the trails near here but not where we just were. We've got the email you sent, Jake, so we've got search parameters and quadrants and will work through some of the other options for where she could be." Caleb was the one who spoke up, but beside him Piper and Adriana nodded.

"You're not going anywhere, right?" Jake turned to Ellie. "You need to get checked out by a doctor, someone with more on hand than antiseptic wipes and Band-Aids." He had more than that in his first aid kit, but still, she needed an actual doctor for wound care.

Ellie nodded. "No arguments here. I'm going to do that, take some Tylenol and get some rest."

"Good. We'll keep communicating with the active searchers," Levi said, looking at the group who was heading back out, "and with you too, Jake, so you know where we are."

And could be kept current on events and potential escalating danger levels. He heard the unsaid words.

"All right."

Jake unlocked his car, let Cassie and Will climb in, which they did wordlessly, and shut the door behind them. Then he turned back to Levi. "I appreciate what you're doing." For the first time, Jake wished he'd gone into law enforcement instead of medicine and rescue. Not because he actually felt his skills would be best used there—no, he was where God wanted him, he knew. But he wished he could be more current with the investigation and be the one on the front lines. He'd have to settle with his friend keeping him updated. And he'd keep his focus on making sure Cassie and Will were safe.

In fact he was already working on ideas for doing just that.

Cassie helped herself to Jake's kitchen and fixed lunch for all three of them. No point in being hungry *and* cooped up in a house that was the last place she would choose to be.

Well, the crosshairs of a potential killer was the last place, but that aside, facing Jake was still one of the hardest things she could think of doing.

Will ate his lunch with only minimal complaints about the bread on his sandwich being wheat instead of white, and then started to yawn. It had been an exhausting day so when Cassie suggested he go lie down to watch a movie, he didn't argue.

A check on him fifteen minutes later revealed what she'd been expecting. He was asleep with his stuffed animal, taken from their bags, which were now in their room. Jake had arranged for a friend to fetch them from the rental car and to take care of getting the vehicle back to a local agency.

Cassie smiled from the doorway of their room, then frowned. The window shade was open, and someone looking from outside could probably see her son stretched out on the bed. Defenseless. She walked into the room, shut the blinds, then looked over at Will. He'd had a scary day. She could only hope rest would help.

Cassie looked away from him and turned to go back downstairs. Jake was right in front of her.

She startled.

"Shh, I'm sorry, I thought you knew I was here. I

didn't mean to scare you." His voice was low, barely above a whisper. Why did it still send shivers straight to Cassie's toes when she hadn't chosen him all those years ago? Surely her abandonment of him and their dreams should have made her reactions to him lessen over the years.

Instead the opposite was true. She was more drawn to him than ever.

"It's okay." She crossed her arms over her chest. He dropped his hands from her shoulders, where they had been, and looked down at the floor.

"He's sleeping?"

She nodded.

"Then we can't put this off anymore, Cassie. We really need to talk."

He'd had time to absorb the news, but she still couldn't read the emotions on his face. His eyes though…those betrayed one bit of his feelings.

He hurt. Worse than if she'd slapped him. *Of course* he hurt. He'd missed out on six years with his son because of her. And still he sheltered them both in his house, and had demonstrated today that he wouldn't hesitate to keep them safe, even if it meant using his body as a shield.

Had she realized when she left exactly what she was walking away from? The fullness of the kind of strong man Jake was? Part of her liked to think that she hadn't known. But no, she had. She'd loved him for every bit of it and she'd still walked away.

And that was part of what told her she was irretrievably broken.

She exhaled, deep. Slow. "Okay, let's talk."

"My office is right there." He motioned to the next

room, the door of which was shut. "If you'd rather be up here next to him than downstairs and farther away."

Cassie felt fairly safe in the house, but she wasn't sure she could trust her judgment anymore about risk. She never would have expected someone to break in the night before and she'd been completely stunned by the attack today. "Yes, let's stay up here."

Jake nodded. "Okay." Then he hesitated. "You go ahead and I'll make us coffee and then come back, okay?"

Cassie wasn't ready for this. But it wasn't fair to him to put it off any longer. She nodded.

The office was pure Jake, a room with a large wooden desk and bookshelves covering every wall. She'd almost forgotten how much he loved to read, for the build of his body made it seem he spent every waking moment outside chasing adventures. He was more well-read than most people, but not pretentious about it. He just genuinely liked gaining knowledge, figuring things out.

She hoped he didn't view this conversation like some kind of fact-finding mission, drilling down into every idea presented, questioning everything. It was the one thing she'd remembered complaining about when they'd dated. He had the meticulousness of someone who'd once wanted to be a doctor, the curious mind of a scientist. And her feelings couldn't always be analyzed or quantified. She'd wanted someone to just…*get* her.

"Here you go." Jake walked in a few minutes later holding two cups of coffee in mugs from Seldovia.

"You finally went, huh?" she asked him. They'd planned to tour the little town near Homer, Alaska, on their honeymoon. The one that had never happened.

Jake shook his head. "No. My parents went and

brought these back as souvenirs and then didn't want to move them when they left the house."

Surely he had more mugs than just these two. And he'd chosen them because…

A nod to their past? The kind meant to cut? Meant to ease the blow of finding out how she'd betrayed him with her secret?

Cassie had to stop analyzing and just wait and see how this went. He had a right to be upset, and she needed to let him start the conversation at his own pace.

It was another time she wished she could pray. But she still couldn't reconcile Jake's faith with the evil she'd had such a firsthand view of lately. How could both exist? Evil go on unchecked?

"So what happened?" he asked as he settled onto one end of the brown leather sofa against the back wall. He kept his voice low and Cassie appreciated it. Will was a hard sleeper, but she didn't want him hearing this conversation, in case he woke up.

"I don't know."

"You have to know."

She did, didn't she? Cassie sighed. "I…"

"Okay, while you think about it, let's start backward. Did you know you were pregnant with him when you left?"

Cassie looked up at him. His jaw was tight, his lips in a straight firm line like he was bracing himself for the damage her words might do.

"No. I didn't know. I never would have left without telling you if I'd known."

He exhaled and sat back against the couch. At least she could give him that much reassurance. What she'd done, not telling him, was inexcusable, but it hadn't been calculated. It just hadn't seemed like news some-one should deliver over the phone, and she hadn't been brave enough to face the situation in person by coming back to Alaska. And she'd been embarrassed. Ashamed. "Okay," Jake said, his voice still steady.

"Everything was going well." Cassie stated what had been obvious to both of them, once upon a time.

Anything in his face that had relaxed tightened again, but there was nothing Cassie could do to change the truth, no matter how much it might hurt.

"It couldn't have been going that well." The first hint of bitterness crept into his tone, one she'd never heard before. Sure, they'd argued. Jake wasn't actually perfect despite the fact that he seemed to be so often, even to her. But this voice was different than any she was fa-miliar with. Harder. Harsher.

"It was." She took a deep breath and reminded her-self not to get defensive. He had every right to be upset by the situation. "It was going well and I loved you, and I was happy."

"Then what happened?"

Cassie hesitated. The life she'd envisioned for her-self hadn't turned out anything like she'd dreamed or planned. So how did she admit she had left him for something that had never materialized? She guessed by just putting one word in front of the other, like the verbal explanations that she needed to offer were foot-steps that had to travel a long way. One step at a time.

"I realized you were going to stay. And I wanted to leave."

"For med school? Cassie, we were both going to leave for medical school. We had a plan."

They'd both been accepted to a good school in Washington, and Jake was right, they'd had the next decade of their lives relatively planned. Undergrad, medical school, residency at schools hopefully close together, but even if they had to be apart, it would be okay because they were strong. Their love would handle the separation.

If only they'd known how the next few years would turn out. How wrong their idealistic hopes in their relationship had been.

"You were always planning to come back, Jake." Cassie kept her voice soft. "You love this town and it loves you back. I...was always just going to be the girl whose mom left her. The one lucky enough to have Jake Stone look her way. I didn't fit here like you did, and I didn't want to try."

"So rather than give me a choice, you just cut and run?"

Cassie hated to admit it, but yes, she'd run. Sometimes running seemed like the best escape route. A truly brave person wouldn't think so. But Cassie had never claimed any extraordinary level of bravery.

"Jake..." she started, but he was shaking his head.

"I tried, Cassie. I tried to come in here and make things comfortable. I tried to do the best I could to handle this." He gestured with his hand between the two of them and toward the room where Will slept. "But that's it? You didn't want to live here? There has to be more."

There wasn't more. Wasn't that enough? The fact that she'd blatantly chosen her dreams over the man she'd promised once to love forever?

And then in a great twist of irony, instead of being a doctor in a big city saving people in an emergency room, she lived in a medium-sized city in Florida—a state she hated, but it had been far from Alaska and her past—working as a pediatric nurse and barely making enough money to pay for the apartment she was raising their son in. Alone.

At the time, she'd felt she was saving Jake as much as herself from future pain. She'd felt her mother's abandonment acutely. She'd known that it was due, at least in part, to her mother wanting more than Raven Pass could offer. What if Cassie was like that too? What if she grew to resent Jake and even her baby for her not being able to leave town and follow her dream? She hadn't wanted to hurt Jake like that, not when she knew what it felt like to be abandoned. So she'd chased her ambitions. Left him behind, even if in her mind she felt like it was what was best for him too.

But dreams sometimes didn't turn out. If her aunt were here, Cassie would complain to her about the fairy tale she'd told her every night when she was a kid, after she and her dad had moved in with her, a story of long-lost love and a princess rescued by a daring hero. She'd wanted to believe that was possible in real life. It wasn't.

"That's all there is." Cassie shrugged. "I was…" Should she tell him the truth? Did it matter anymore? She didn't want another chance with him because she didn't deserve it and he deserved better. But something in her wanted to come completely clean. "I was wrong, Jake. And I'm sorry." Then she set her half-empty mug of lukewarm coffee down on the table by the sofa, and walked to her room without another word.

SIX

Jake had thought Cassie would eventually have to come out of the room she and Will were staying in. But she stayed there for the entire afternoon and long enough past a normal dinnertime that he finally had to admit she wasn't going to face him. At least not today. He suspected, after all the tension of the day, she'd fallen asleep.

The explanations she'd given him felt hollow, left him feeling worse than he had before. Somehow he'd always imagined there was some big reason, something that justified shattering their future without his input.

He moved to the back windows, looking outside and making sure nothing out there gave him cause for alarm. Next window, same thing. He couldn't shake the fear that someone was going to come after her again. It was *when*, not *if*. And he wanted her safe even if she'd broken his heart. Back then and now. He'd gone into today expecting to feel better somehow, to understand. Instead the truth was empty. She hadn't talked to him back then about her dreams, or her concerns, had left instead, and neither of them could get the last seven years back. Even if they wanted to. And after something like this…

Still, he knew not all the blame lay on her. Not really. She'd called him not long after she left and he hadn't taken her call. Had she been trying to tell him then?

She hadn't even brought that attempt up in her defense, he'd noticed. She was perfectly happy to take all the blame. But the truth was, she had reached out. In a small way, but still, she'd tried.

And he'd been too hurt to answer, then too upset to call back.

So they'd both helped destroy what they'd had.

Jake knew he'd still probably love her forever, would maybe never be able to settle down with anyone because every woman he'd tried to show interest in was a poor substitute for what he really wanted—*who* he wanted. But he was finally willing to admit they weren't good for each other and had maybe never been meant to be together.

If only they'd figured that out back then and come to a mutual decision. If only he'd stuck to the truths he'd known were right and honored her the way he should have.

But Will was a blessing, wasn't he? He couldn't bring himself to wish the kid out of existence. His son. No, Will was something out of this whole experience to be thankful for. He'd rather have his son and be missing seven years of his life than not have him at all.

God, I don't know how You're going to work this out. Can You fix this kind of pain? No, I'm sorry, Lord, I know You can. But will You?

Jake heard nothing in reply.

He made himself a sandwich. Ate it, and then called Caleb. He'd said he could give him some backup if necessary, and Jake needed at least a few hours of sleep.

* * *

Just past one in the morning, Jake got up, fully awake. He reached for his phone, thinking it may have roused him. No missed calls or messages. He'd expected one of the police officers to want to talk more. He'd have to call in a few hours, when people were starting morning shifts. Before he'd fallen asleep, he'd been thinking about Will and wondering if there wasn't some way to separate him from Cassie and keep him safe. She wouldn't like it, he knew, but it was starting to seem like the best option.

He was Will's dad. He had some rights too, which was another thing Cassie was going to have to talk to him about. He wanted to be in his son's life.

Even if he had to leave Alaska?

He tried the question on for size. He loved his work with the rescue team and wasn't sure how he'd make a living and provide for his son otherwise. So quitting full-on wasn't an option for him...but part of the year? He could make sacrifices in order to really get to know Will, have his son know him.

Sleep wasn't going to come back, not with thoughts like these going through his mind right now. Jake threw back the covers, then pulled on jeans and a shirt. Besides, this way Caleb, who was downstairs on the couch, could get some sleep. Jake appreciated his friend giving him some much-needed backup, but he was okay now.

He opened the door to his room, then walked down the hall, pausing outside Cassie and Will's room.

Opening the door was probably some kind of violation of privacy. But now that he'd had some rest and could think clearly, his protectiveness—and the fears that went with it—kicked in. Was there a chance they'd been attacked last night and that's why she hadn't come down? He didn't think so; he'd heard nothing.

But now that the thought had popped into his mind, the worry vibrated inside him, wouldn't let go.

He eased the door open.

Will was asleep on the bed, sprawled across it, his small hand across the pillow next to him.

Cassie. Jake's heart thudded and he blinked in case his eyes weren't seeing something in the darkness.

"You should really let someone know if you're going to check on them in the middle of the night. You could scare them otherwise."

Cassie's voice. She was curled up in the chair by the window, a blanket over her huddled form.

"I'm sorry. I just needed to know you were okay." Jake didn't regret his decision to come in. Surely she understood that their protection was a higher priority than dancing around whatever propriety demanded at the moment.

"I'm fine. Sorry I worried you." She shifted in the chair. "Will was taking up the whole bed and I didn't want to wake him, so I've been sleeping here."

"Sleeping?" She sounded awake to him.

Cassie shrugged. "Enough. Off and on. You're not the only one worried." Her eyes went to the window, maybe subconsciously. Jake hated that the threat weighed on her at all hours, but he was glad she wasn't letting her guard down. It was safer that way.

"Okay, well, I'm sorry. Glad you're all right." Jake moved for the door.

"Jake?"

He swallowed hard. Stopped walking. Something in

her voice sounded like their past, guard down, years erased. It tugged at him. "Yeah?"

"I'm sorry."

Not just for tonight, but for more than that. He could tell by the weight of her whisper.

"I know." He hesitated. "I forgive you." And he did, for keeping Will away from him, even for hurting him in the past. But if there was one thing the last day had made clear to him, it was that they'd had their chance and anything between them was over. For the sake of their son though, he had to live his faith and let go of any bitterness over the lost years with Will. His faith taught him love was the most important path in life. He loved Will.

All these years he'd thought he wanted a second chance with Cassie. While he'd always love her, maybe what he'd really needed was forgiveness. For both of them.

"And I'm sorry too," he said, for whatever had gone wrong that was also his fault, for the choices he'd made that had led to Cassie thinking she had to leave.

"Thanks, Jake."

He walked out the door and down the stairs, ready to keep watch the rest of the night. He certainly wasn't going to be sleeping anymore.

When Jake reached the living room, Caleb looked up at him, questions on his face.

"Everything's fine," Jake said, though it was debatable if it was true. He and Cassie were both broken inside, he knew that, from past hurts. Maybe tonight was a step toward healing but neither of them was fine yet, not in Jake's opinion. But Caleb would be curious about how things were going safety-wise.

"Good. Are you planning to stay up now?"

"Yeah, I'm done sleeping. Do you want to head up to the other guest room to crash or go home?"

"Upstairs is fine. I've been walking a lot to stay awake and keep an eye on things outside. So far nothing seems out of the ordinary."

Jake was thankful for it, he just wasn't taking chances after the night before. "Thanks for the help."

He took the spot on the couch his friend vacated, thoughts still running wild. He reached for the table by the sofa and eased open the drawer and pulled out a notebook. He might not be able to get much done with the case now in the middle of the night, but he could make some notes to remember for tomorrow.

Priority number one was finding somewhere safe for Will to go, at least during the day. Cassie wasn't going to let him out of her sight at night, that had been clear after checking on her. Jake might be trying to keep both of them safe, but as far as Cassie was concerned, she was the one watching over the kid. He could respect that. But during the day Cassie might still want to help, now that there was a tenuous peace between them again. Surely there was an option that would work for everyone.

He broached the subject with Cassie that morning while pouring her coffee. He'd used the French press this morning, which was her favorite, or at least it used to be.

"We need to talk about Will."

"What about him?" Her tone was guarded, and he didn't blame her. Yesterday's conversation… It could have gone better.

Jake shook his head and poured himself some cereal. "Nothing big, sorry if it sounded that way."

Cassie opened the cabinet with the bowls and grabbed two of them, then reached for the cereal when he was done. It was the kind of early morning routine couples did all the time, and it affected Jake more than he would have thought it would. It was surreal, still, to have her in his house like this. Like a little flicker of an idea for how it might have been if not for all that had gone wrong.

"Okay, what then?" she asked.

"He's got to stay with someone else during the day."

"No."

"Cassie, you were there yesterday. It was dangerous and I don't want it to happen again. He doesn't need to be exposed to a threat like that."

"I agree, but I'm the best one to protect him."

"Are you?" He let a few beats pass and watched her face. Her expressions flickered from one end of the emotional spectrum to the other until she finally seemed to settle on cautious.

"Tell me what you had in mind."

"I called the police chief this morning and explained the situation to him. His son-in-law is a police officer also and is on leave this week to spend time at home with his family. They offered to let Will stay with them where someone can make sure he's not in the line of fire." Not that he was expecting any more firing. He was certainly hoping there wouldn't be, but as yesterday had proved, it was better to assume the worst.

Cassie nodded, but still didn't say anything. She looked back toward the stairs, like she was thinking of Will, and left the empty bowl and the cereal on the counter. He was still asleep, Jake guessed. Her own bowl she carried to the table and sat down, then started to eat.

So was she still thinking, or...? The Cassie he'd known was confident, bold, which meant she usually responded immediately and had her mind made up quickly.

Then again, she'd made her mind up quickly and told him no, hadn't she? So maybe it was best that she took a little more time to think it through. Jake had confidence in her as a mom, but this was an area where he knew he could help, or at least connect her with people who could.

"It's for the best, Cassie," he said quietly, as he walked toward her, not meaning for her name to come off of his lips quite so gently. She couldn't tell, could she, how much he still cared by his tone? He hoped not, because any ridiculous feelings he had didn't need to be acted upon. He knew that.

Then she was facing him, her bright green eyes searching his. "You really think so?"

The idea that she cared what he thought made his heart beat faster even as the alarm bells in his brain went off. He couldn't care that she cared, couldn't let himself get close again.

It's already going to hurt enough when she leaves, with your son, he reminded himself. But he couldn't quite pull his eyes away from hers. He nodded, slowly. "Yes."

Her lips parted and he fought to pull his eyes away from them. She sighed. "Okay."

"Okay? You'll let him stay with them?" he clarified.

Cassie nodded. "Yes. I still want to help and you're right, his staying with me is putting him in too much danger. Even if I stayed here during the day, he's probably still safer with an officer's family than with me and I want what's best for him, not just what I want."

"Great." He looked away from her, and whatever moment they'd had had passed. "We'll take him there this morning and then you and I will head out with the team."

She nodded, then focused her attention back on her cereal.

Jake took a deep breath and asked God to help them find her aunt, preferably today.

SEVEN

Will had been more than cooperative at the idea of playing with new friends during the day instead of being with his mom, Cassie thought. Of course, he was six now, not nearly so interested in her whereabouts and spending time with her as he had been at five. Every year seemed to bring more longing for independence from him, and made it clearer to her that boys needed their dads, whenever it was possible.

She needed to tell Will. Jake hadn't pressured her about it, though he had to have it on his mind, she thought as they pulled away from the police officer's house in Jake's car. She appreciated the way he'd handled this.

Perfectly.

No surprise there.

They met up with the team in a parking lot farther from her aunt's house than the trailhead where they'd met yesterday. But Cassie knew from the time she'd spent living and hiking in Raven Pass that it was basically the third point of a triangle, with the other two being her aunt's house and the trailhead from the day before. She hadn't seen any maps, but she assumed the search team must have some since they'd talked about breaking into areas to search.

"So are you guys still thinking my idea could be right, that she hiked from her house on one of her normal trails and then something happened?"

Jake didn't answer right away. Cassie turned to look at him, noticing that the expression on his face was nothing short of grim.

"You don't think it was an accident though, her disappearance," she surmised, not needing verbal confirmation anymore. His facial expression had given her enough.

"They're working it as a murder investigation. That's what Levi Wicks went over again when he called."

"He called you and talked about it?"

"Yes, he's my friend and he knew I wanted to know."

"Well she is my aunt, so you should have told me. I would think you'd have a basic sense of decency and know that without needing to be told." Cassie felt her voice rising, felt her mind telling her to stop talking before she dug herself any further into a hole with Jake, who had really shown her a lot of grace since she'd been back in town.

"I would have thought you'd have the decency to actually say goodbye before leaving town and not coming back for over half a decade, but here we are." His voice had lowered, but it wasn't intimidating. Jake had never yelled at her and apparently wouldn't start even now. But it was flat. Devoid of any warmth.

Cassie was sorry for what she'd done, but she'd already said so. It hurt for him to throw it in her face like this, and she wondered if this would evolve into some kind of never-ending penance. Cassie made mistakes, and she apologized or learned from them, and then she moved on. She knew this particular mistake was bigger than most, and she knew Jake had a right to be angry, that moving on from it might take a little longer. But she hoped he wouldn't keep using it as punishment.

Wasn't that the whole problem with Jake in the first place though, his inability to move on? His well-sunk roots into Raven Pass soil made it impossible to go on to the next adventure, like Cassie had always longed to do.

He didn't like change. He'd probably never get past this, the hurt she'd caused him, either. For the last few days she'd wondered how he could so easily forgive her and act like the past hadn't happened. In a way it had seemed too good to be true, but it was Jake and he'd always seemed that way to her.

Now at least she knew. He hadn't forgiven her.

She met his eyes, nodded once. At least she knew where they stood. "Let's go."

He climbed out of the vehicle without another word and they started hiking, through the big meadow where the trailhead started, and toward the tall spruce trees that seemed to swallow up the trail without a hint of where it was going. But Cassie knew the way, even if she and Jake got separated.

She'd be fine. With or without him.

Just like she always had been.

Jake didn't mean to be setting a pace worthy of some kind of sports-conditioning program, but he'd always worked off frustrations with exercise, and *frustration* didn't begin to describe what he was feeling right now. With himself, with Cassie.

He squeezed his eyes shut for an instant and tried to

pray but he was still too upset, all his boiling emotions too close to the surface.

One foot in front of the other. Another step and another, his hiking boots pounding the ground. Cassie was upset about her aunt. She was in danger, which wasn't something she was accustomed to. There were all kinds of excuses and explanations for her behavior and the hurtful words she'd said, but had he accepted any of that? No, he'd just exploded in a low-voiced sentence of words designed to hurt.

They'd hurt her. And he was sorry.

She wasn't ready to hear that yet though, so he just punished himself with a pace that made him more out of breath than he'd been in years. She kept up fine, and he wondered what she had been doing to keep in such good shape.

Not that it surprised him. She'd always been able to match him and she'd never been the kind of woman who made Jake feel like he had to wait for her. No, Cassie could handle herself fine in any environment and it was part of why he'd fallen in love with her in the first place.

She kept pace with him for another ten minutes, as they wound through the spruce on a side trail so narrow he wasn't sure he'd have found it without her direction. It was then he started to notice that she was getting out of breath and he slowed. Rain had begun to fall; some was even finding its way down through the tree canopy.

"I'm sorry," he said, knowing she'd know what for. She'd always been able to read his mind, or at least it had seemed that way, and with how little had changed between the two of them, he suspected that hadn't changed either. The raindrops on the tree limbs were the only sound for a few seconds until she finally spoke up.

Cassie nodded. "Me too."

Jake stopped walking and gently turned Cassie to face him, his hands on her upper arms. "You've already apologized for what you did." He looked her in the eyes. "Another apology isn't needed and I'm sorry I made you feel as though it was."

He'd only wanted to face her so she could see his expression and know how sincere he was about her not needing to apologize anymore. He hadn't meant to fling an accusation at her, and he intended to keep a check on the emotions that had fed that outburst. She didn't deserve that.

The two of them facing each other like this had made the world almost still, except the gentle sound of the rain, the way it was falling on the curls that usually edged around Cassie's face when she was wearing a ponytail. It was dangerous, feeling like he and Cassie were the only two people on earth, and the only two people in this stretch of Alaskan woods.

Chemistry had never been an issue between them. They'd always had more than Jake had known how to handle.

Jake caught his breath, didn't move. He knew all the reasons he should be careful not to give her the impression they could pick up where they left off because they couldn't.

Cassie moved closer, her eyes on his lips, her chin tilted up.

Her lips met his and it was like all the yesterdays were gone and they were back, six years ago, lips touching just like this. Gentle, tentative and then bolder.

She'd been his once and this kiss said that she still

was, somehow, despite the mistakes, the years, the regrets.

Jake kissed her with every ounce of himself that had missed her over the years, and she responded.

Nothing had ended between them then at all. They'd been put on pause.

Jake slowed his kiss, had to make himself pull away, because this wasn't the time or place. They separated and he had to catch his breath.

"If you apologize for that I may never speak to you again." Cassie's voice was breathless too and Jake squeezed his eyes shut, loving the sound of it, the memory of her lips on his.

"Later. We have to talk about that later," he said quietly.

Cassie didn't answer.

"Seriously, Cassie."

She finally nodded. "Okay. We'll talk later."

Jake swallowed hard, unable to formulate any more words at the moment. His train of thought had certainly narrowed, to Cassie and loving her, kissing her, spending the rest of his life with her...

His mind tried to caution him from letting his heart carry his thoughts away because he'd tried this once and had never been the same after. But at the moment he had no desire to listen to the caution. Instead he grabbed her hand, squeezed it gently while he met her eyes and then nodded, like a promise.

And hoped that this one would turn out better than the promises they'd made last time.

Cassie couldn't breathe, couldn't think. Jake had kissed her. No, she realized, as she ducked around a bush of salmonberries, she'd kissed Jake. He hadn't moved away, and he'd been a willing…participant…in the entire kiss, but she'd started it.

Oh, how she'd started it. And with it she'd restarted all kinds of worries and fears in her mind. It had been easier, in a way, to pretend the spark between the two of them had died, that she'd killed it all those years ago, but clearly that was a lie.

Cassie just didn't know what to do about it, here and now today. So talking about it wasn't something that was high on her list of priorities, but she knew Jake was right. They had to talk.

If she'd talked to him before she left, like he'd mentioned earlier, how different would things have turned out? Would they have really had a happily-ever-after, living in Jake's parents' house together, married like they'd planned, with Will and a little sibling maybe? Her heart squeezed and she had to blink back the tears edging over the corners of her eyes. You couldn't go back. Wasn't that what she'd been telling herself for years now?

Except it almost looked like she had the chance now. Would she take it? Could she?

Cassie felt adrift and wondered if this was one of those times that Jake would pray and if she could learn to.

Um, God, we could use help figuring out what to do, she tried as a tentative test.

She didn't hear anything back, but she did feel her shoulders relax a little. *Huh*.

They hiked on without talking, taking game trail after game trail, winding so deep into the woods that Cassie was getting nervous and hoping she could find their way back out. This part of the woods had been one of her favorite spots as a child, for the way the wilderness seemed to swallow a person whole. For that same reason now, Cassie felt her muscles tensing, her heartbeat growing faster. Fear had crept out of the corners of her mind, where it had been temporarily banished while she'd been kissing Jake, and had taken a more front and center spot now. It washed over her and she wasn't able to stop or even slow it. Goose bumps shivered down her arms and she could almost smell fear.

No, not fear. Something else.

"Jake." She stopped walking, her nose registering immediately what took her mind a few moments to realize.

The smell was decay. And how many people walked this way or used this trail?

She'd feared her aunt was dead and had wondered if the hurt could actually get worse if it was really true. It could. It did. Despair hung on her like a too heavy blanket, scratchy and hard.

And then Cassie moved to the side of the trail to throw up. Jake kept walking.

"Stay there," he told her, pulling his .44 from his chest holster and handing it to her once she'd stood up and regained a tiny bit of equilibrium. "Use this if you need to."

He had taught her to shoot with either this one or one very similar when they were in high school. Cassie nodded and sat down, a few feet away from where she'd been sick, in the shelter of some berry bushes.

Her aunt had loved salmonberries. That was probably why this had been one of her favorite trails. When Cassie was a kid, they used to walk this trail and pick them together, and then her aunt would make jam.

Her aunt was gone.

Why had Cassie left?

It was too late to fix any of it, her regrets about the

time spent away, all the years she'd said she'd visit one day and hadn't. Cassie had let her aunt down, let herself down.

Tears threatened to overtake her, but fear kept them at bay for now. Because one other question wouldn't leave her alone no matter how much she tried to think about other aspects of what was going on.

If Jake and the police were right and her aunt hadn't died of natural causes, then someone had wanted her dead.

Why?

And if they'd done that as intended, why would they come after Cassie? She had nothing they could want, barely any money in her savings, and what she would inherit from her aunt amounted to the tiny cottage on half an acre. Nothing worth killing over.

It didn't make sense.

Cassie lowered her head and cried.

EIGHT

Jake had seen his share of people who had died. It was part of being a paramedic and on a search-and-rescue team. And in a small town, he had even seen people die whom he'd known in life. But seeing Cassie's aunt crumpled among a patch of fireweed shattered him. Cassie's sobs in the distance wrenched his gut. He felt the pain and weight of her hurt almost like it was his own.

Because it was. He did hurt when she hurt. Always had. Because he loved her.

Jake bit back a groan. Another realization he wasn't ready to face, and it had to take a back seat for now since dealing with the fallout of this discovery took priority. He pulled his phone from his pocket. No service. He took the backpack off, eased the SAT phone out of the top pocket and dialed Levi's number. Jake's team was out searching, and they would be his second call, but he figured law enforcement should know first. And the sooner the Raven Pass Police Department got here, the sooner Jake could leave and take Cassie with him. He was worried about her, and more than just emotionally. It wasn't unheard of for someone to go into legitimate medical shock after an event like this and he wanted to avoid that with Cassie if he could.

"I found her." He kept his voice low. "Near Bold Mountain, on the side closest to town."

Levi asked a few more questions about location, her condition.

"Dead, and not recently." The smell was unbearable. Jake couldn't bear to look at her and hadn't even needed to take her pulse to confirm that she was dead. He then gave Levi directions to the trailhead and their location.

"I'll be there as fast as I can. You don't have to stay right there next to the body. Living people take priority and Cassie's still in danger so get her somewhere sheltered nearby."

"I'll do that," Jake promised.

He next call was to Caleb, to whom he told the same information, but faster since he was walking back to Cassie and eager to focus on her.

"You okay, man?" Caleb asked.

Jake couldn't remember really *needing* his teammates for anything personal before. He knew he could count on them during a search and didn't hesitate to put his life in their hands. But he hadn't really talked to them much about his personal life or counted on them to care about it.

The fact that all of them seemed…sensitive to his current situation was unusual. But he appreciated it.

"I think so. Thanks for asking."

He ended the call and made his way back to Cassie. Or tried to. He didn't see her anywhere, and the tall fireweed and other vegetation obscured her from view.

If she was still there at all.

Could it have been a trap, Cassie's aunt's body being

right there where they could see it? Had whoever killed her meant for Cassie to find the body and then planned to overpower her in her grief? His heart pounded faster as he scanned the area and then started using his hands to press weeds to the side so he could see better. Where had she been?

"Cassie?"

He waited. Nothing. The panic that had been growing exploded in his chest and Jake realized again how much things weren't over between them. Not even close. "Cassie!" Louder this time.

"Here. I'm down here." She stood up, unfolding herself from her place among the brush, about fifteen feet farther than where he was standing. Her face was red, tears under her eyes smudged with some kind of makeup. Mascara, maybe. Cassie sniffed.

"It's her, right? And she's really gone?"

Jake nodded, slowly. He couldn't bring himself to say the words out loud, but the nod seemed to be enough for Cassie to have to fight back a fresh round of sobs.

"Sweetheart…" His words betrayed him, but he ignored it and held out his arms. This wasn't the time to think of all the reasons they couldn't be together.

There were some of those, weren't there?

Still, not the time. Cassie moved toward him and he wrapped his arms around her as she pressed herself against him and cried into his shoulder, like she was giving her tears to him to carry. Jake just stood there, held her for another few minutes before he remembered what Levi had told him to do.

And he hoped he wasn't too late.

"We can't stay right here, Cassie. Levi is worried about your safety. The fact that your aunt is dead doesn't put you in less danger. If anything, the danger is worse now because whoever killed her won't hesitate to kill again. It's a sort of point of no return."

Cassie nodded, brushing away the wetness from her eyes. "Okay, where?"

Jake looked around the meadow. They could sit down like she'd been doing and probably not be seen, but he wasn't as comfortable with that option. It wasn't defensible. They'd be better off among the trees.

"This way." He unwrapped his arms from her, but didn't break contact as he slid his hand down her arm and then grasped her hand in his.

He felt her flinch a little. Met her eyes. "Is this okay or should I let go?" He swallowed hard, the charge between them almost a tangible thing.

Cassie nodded. "Don't let go." Her words were almost softer than a whisper. But firm.

He didn't let go.

They hurried together through the tall plants, toward the edge of the forest but not in the direction they'd come from. Jake wanted to be off the trail, even though it wasn't a very obvious trail, just to make their chances better.

"Here is good." He motioned to the base of an old spruce, whose branches tangled in such way that they'd be sheltered from the back, more or less, but have their view to the front open to the meadow and only slightly obscured by the tall vegetation.

Cassie nodded and sank down beside him, laying her head on his shoulder.

"Jake… Thanks."

He nodded.

She looked up, tears in her eyes. "Do you know how… she died?"

"No. Looks like a blow to the head, but we don't know if she fell or if someone hit her. The coroner will let us know eventually."

She rested there, quietly, warm against him, not speaking, just staying in the moment.

She lifted a hand to his chest as she leaned closer to him.

Jake held his breath, tried not to move. It had been so long since she'd touched him like that, since he'd felt so close to another soul.

And she was grieving. Not thinking clearly.

He moved her hand away. Cleared his throat. "No matter what, I'm glad I could be here. We…we should never have stopped being friends at least. I'm glad I can be one for you now."

And he felt her pull away, not physically. Her head was still on his shoulder. But he felt the tension gather in her body, the stiffness in her shoulders.

He could have sat there forever, forgetting the present and living in the past, maybe making one of his old mistakes all over again if she'd asked him to. But he wasn't that man anymore, and didn't want to be. God had forgiven him for the past, but he wanted to do better in the future, not just for him, but for Cassie.

Or…whoever he ended up with.

Because maybe there was just too much between them to be able to move on. Maybe they'd had their chance.

Maybe all he could hope for now was the chance to keep her safe and one day get to know his son.

Maybe second chances didn't happen after all.

* * *

Cassie had stayed curled up against Jake, willing herself to get the strength to pull away from him, but she couldn't. Even if he'd made it clear where they stood, emphasized the fact that they were *friends*, which apparently nullified that earlier kiss, she still felt stronger when she was with him and she wasn't sure she could withstand the onslaught of her circumstances right now without him beside her.

So she did the easy thing and stayed still, even though it broke her heart a little more because it reminded her of the love with Jake she could never have. But what was another crack in a heart that was already broken beyond repair?

The police eventually arrived. Cassie and Jake watched them from afar until they could see Officer Wicks—Levi, she was beginning to call him in her mind, like Jake did—looking around, like he was trying to find them. Then they emerged from their cover and walked to where he was.

Cassie didn't pay attention to what the men said, even though she did want to know what had happened to her aunt. Instead, here in the moment, all she could do was breathe and listen to the rhythm of her heart whooshing in her ears. *She's gone. She's gone. She's gone.*

By the time Jake steered her back to the trail and said something about how they were free to leave, the rhythm had progressed to a full-on migraine, her head pounding along with her heart. Her stomach felt queasy again, but not the kind being sick could ease.

God, why?

They walked the trail down silently. Cassie led them back the way they'd come, surprised at how easily the directions came to her again. It was like she'd traveled this trail hundreds of times in her memory, not just the a-couple-times-a-year treks with her aunt to pick berries. Strange. Or a side effect of grief sharpening her mind and memory? Cassie didn't know.

"Do you want to go home?" Jake asked in the trail-head parking lot. There were police cruisers there; one of them was parked next to Jake's car. The officer there nodded to them and even in her mental fog, Cassie appreciated that men had been stationed there to make sure no one was lying in wait at the car or had rigged it to hurt them somehow.

"No," Cassie surprised herself by saying. "I want to go to my aunt's house."

Jake nodded, adding no words. She knew the police had finished their investigation there already.

Cassie heard Jake on the phone, checking on Will. That made sense; it was much later than they'd planned to be done. Almost dinnertime.

She couldn't imagine being hungry.

The drive there didn't take long, and Cassie kept her attention to things outside the windows rather than have to face Jake and talk to him. It wasn't the most crushing blow of the night—his reminder that what they had was friendship at best—but it was another blow when she didn't feel like she could take any more.

When they pulled into the driveway, the door to the house was still open.

"Don't the police usually fix doors? Or put crime-scene tape up?" Cassie mumbled, her mind focusing enough to get the questions out.

"Stay here." Jake reached for the door handle, then turned back to her and she understood. He didn't want to leave her. She was tired of this, tired of wondering what was a trap and when she should go with him and when she should stay, and she was exhausted and grieving. And. She. Could. Not. Do. This. Anymore.

Of course she didn't have a choice, so she took a deep breath and got out too. "I can go with you. I can do this."

Did he believe the words any more than she did? She stepped from the truck, exhaustion making her sore down to her bones. Again, she wished she could trust God. But she couldn't.

Right? Maybe it was a subject that deserved more consideration and thought from her. But all she knew was that Jake was holding himself together well. A friend of hers she'd known years ago when they competed in high school running events in the state—Summer Dawson—had gone through a scary time a few years ago but had seemingly held it together fine. And Cassie knew she was a Christian, like Jake was. Could it be that easy? Trust that someone else was in control and then you didn't have to carry the weight of everything on your own?

Cassie walked toward the front door, gravel crunching under her feet as all the times she'd done this before, walked to her aunt's home, paraded in her mind like a newsreel of memories. She'd seen her aunt for the last time. Talked to her for the last time.

So many lasts. So little hope.

"This shouldn't be like this," Jake muttered as he looked closer at the door. He shook his head. "Back to the car. I wanted to see for sure before we called anyone, but this is new."

Cassie walked back to the vehicle, her mind waking up a little more and kicking into gear to remind her to be aware of her surroundings. Will needed her. She couldn't let her guard down, not even now.

Jake put the car in gear once they were both inside and he'd ended his phone call to the police. Cassie wasn't even buckled yet; she'd thought they were waiting for the police to arrive. "What are you doing?"

"Not sitting here with you in the car like a stationary target, that's for sure." He shook his head once, seriousness etched on his features. Today had taken a lot out of him too, Cassie could see, now that she was paying attention. So maybe the trusting-God concept wasn't a cure-all. How did it work then?

She wanted to ask Jake, but not today, not after how close they'd been, only to find herself ripped away from him again, this time not from her own choice to run, but from his intentional distancing by calling them *friends* so pointedly.

Instead she said nothing, just looked out the window as they rode around town. Jake pulled out his phone again. It didn't seem to be synced with any Bluetooth, so Cassie frowned and waited to hear whom he was talking to.

"Hey, it's Jake. Everything still okay there? There's been another break-in at Mabel Hawkins's house. It's likely whoever is behind all of this is still in town, so I just wanted to make sure… Yeah, I know you know what you're doing. Overprotective. Yeah, maybe. I've never had a kid before. Pretty sure when there's a crazy criminal in your kid's town that's linked to his family, paranoia is expected. All right, thanks, man. I appreciate it."

Ah, the officer who was letting Will stay at his house.

"He's okay?" Cassie confirmed.

Jake nodded.

"Yes, and I told him…you know, about Will being my son. Just to make sure he understands how important his safety is to me."

At least she was thankful for the fact that the search yesterday hadn't led to her aunt's body. In retrospect, that was another reason she shouldn't have brought him with her the day before. Even though she'd hoped her aunt wasn't dead, she knew it had been a possibility, and Will being present for that would have scarred him.

Thank you. She found herself whispering to a God whom she'd mentally debated the existence and trustworthiness of a hundred times over. But she still felt compelled somehow to talk to Him. Odd.

"Why is this happening?" she asked against her better judgment as they made another turn on a side street and Jake glanced at the dashboard clock. The police must have told him how many minutes it would take to get to her aunt's house, and he was killing time until then.

Bad phrase. *Wasting* time.

"This with your aunt?" Jake seemed surprised at the question. "We don't know, Cassie. They're still compiling ideas so far, and motive and opportunity and all that kind of stuff."

Here was her chance to just keep quiet, not follow through with the conversation she knew she wasn't ready to have. Not with him, when it involved opening herself up and making herself vulnerable by admitting she might be wrong about something as important and personal as faith. "Not about that." She heard herself keep talking before she'd consciously decided to. "*Why* the grand scheme? Don't you believe God has a plan? How could this fit?"

He didn't answer. For a minute she wasn't sure if she'd offended him.

"I don't know." His words were barely audible. They were pulling back into her aunt's driveway and a squad car was out front, reminding her again that this wasn't fair.

She certainly didn't know how it could possibly make sense, but she'd thought Jake would have an answer. Wasn't that what faith did? Gave a person answers?

"What do you mean? You don't *know*?"

"Trusting God doesn't mean He explains Himself to me, Cassie. There's a verse in the Bible about how His thoughts aren't ours and His ways aren't ours. Somewhere in Isaiah, I think. So no, I don't know why this would happen." He put the car in Park. "I wish it hadn't. But I'm not God and He has a plan."

Hmm. It wasn't the too-easy explanation she'd been anticipating, been ready to shoot down. She knew better than to believe that life came with easy answers. Maybe she'd been hoping he would offer her some so she could continue to discount his faith like she'd done before.

How much had their difference of opinion in that regard played into her decision to leave? She'd never wondered before, but didn't have time to follow up on the thought now, as a police officer she hadn't met yet was waving them over to the house.

"Who is that?" she asked as she followed Jake there. He looked familiar.

"Judah Wicks. He's Levi's brother and also a police officer."

That explained why she'd thought she'd met him. He did look something like his brother, but broader and taller and a bit more serious. Levi smiled more. This guy had no laugh lines.

"Jake, thanks for calling this in," he said as they approached. "And you're Cassie?"

"Yes. Cassie Hawkins, nice to meet you." Manners kicked in automatically and Cassie felt an unexpected stab of pain. Her dad hadn't taught her manners. That had been her aunt's doing. As a kid she hadn't realized how much responsibility her aunt had voluntarily taken on when she offered to have her brother and niece move in. It had changed Cassie's life for the better, but what an adjustment her single aunt must have had to make.

And did I ever even say thank you?

"So what's going on?"

"I've done a quick look around the house. There's a mess, but it's safe. Structurally sound, nothing I can see as far as danger. I'd like Cassie to walk through it with me to see if she can help me identify if anything is missing. Last time it was broken into and someone made a mess we chalked it up to a fit of rage of some kind. Now that someone has returned and done the same thing, we need to try to figure out why they were here," Judah Wicks explained.

Cassie nodded. "I'll do it." Any way she could help. The drive to be involved had grown stronger with the knowledge that her aunt was dead. Maybe it was some kind of desire for revenge, which of course she wasn't going to get, but being involved would make it feel more like she played a part in bringing whoever had done this to justice, and Cassie wanted that. Badly.

"If she goes, I'm going."

Judah raised his eyebrows but nodded at Jake without hesitation. "Of course."

As though she needed Jake there for protection when she was walking around the house with a man who had a gun on his hip and a build that would dwarf a great number of NFL players. It was sweet of him to want to be there though. Although she couldn't understand why he'd go to so much trouble for someone he'd pointedly called a *friend* just a few hours before.

Judah stopped them both inside the front door and handed them each a pair of nitrile gloves. "Put these on. We're still waiting for a forensics team to come out from another town, so we don't want you compromising fingerprints. Ideally you'll touch as little as possible, but just in case."

They both pulled the gloves on.

The living room was a mess, Cassie discovered as they stepped inside, and she looked to the left. The kitchen and dining room, on her right and opened to the main living space, were messy but not quite as bad. Drawers had been opened and left haphazardly with no pattern. She'd heard once that professional thieves knew to start with the bottom drawers so they wouldn't have to close drawers behind themselves, but this wasn't professional if that was the case. Some drawers were pushed in almost all the way, some were fully open and some were in between.

Someone had been looking for something.

But what?

NINE

Jake followed Cassie, careful not to get in her way or distract her. She seemed more focused now than she had been earlier, though he wasn't sure if that was a good thing. Earlier she'd been in full self-protection mode. Even though it hurt him to see her that way, he wasn't sure it wasn't best for her.

Now she was prepared to help however she could. He was proud of her. Scared for her. Frustrated beyond all reason that he couldn't get his head straight when it came to her, no matter how much he tried.

"What were they looking for?" Cassie asked Judah.

Judah raised his eyebrows. "Why do you assume they were looking for something? Do you know what it could be?"

Jake liked Judah fine most of the time, though he was closer to his brother. But he didn't like the way the man was practically implying that Cassie had something to hide, or knew more about this than she was saying. While she frowned, Jake jumped in.

"Of course she doesn't know. She's asking you be-cause she looked around and saw the signs. Her aunt was already gone by the time someone did this. Obviously they were looking for something."

Judah shot him a warning look. "I'm asking Cassie."

She threw Jake a glance that indicated she appreciated his support. She'd been hard to read today, leaning up against him one minute and freezing him out the next. He couldn't figure her out.

And he didn't need to. They weren't a couple, weren't even close anymore.

So clearly following her around the house like she needed him was a logical thing to do.

"Anything missing that you've noticed yet?" Judah asked Cassie, giving Jake a sort of warning look that wasn't necessary. He wasn't planning to say anything else.

Cassie shook her head and moved from the main living area into a hallway. She hesitated in front of the study and then walked in. "This is a mess."

It was an understatement. The desk drawers had been haphazardly opened and half closed like in the other rooms, and there were books all over the floor, some open, pages fluttering, some shut, all of them piled up at least a foot high on the floor.

The shelves were empty.

Had someone flown into a rage and destroyed the order on the bookshelves for no reason? Jake didn't know how to analyze something like that and wasn't convinced Judah was equipped to either. It seemed like something a forensic psychologist would need to work on.

"Why would someone mess with her books?" Cassie frowned and moved toward them, bending down by the pile. She slipped one back onto the shelf and then looked up at Judah. "Am I allowed to fix these? I mean, they're not like evidence, are they?"

"You can fix them. We'll fingerprint them in case, but I doubt the placement of the books matters."

Cassie kept setting them on the shelves, book after book, until the floor was clear. Jake didn't remember going into this room before when he'd been invited to her aunt's house, so he felt like it must have been a special room for her. He understood Cassie's desire to straighten it up.

She was lining up the front covers of the last couple of books with the rest of their row and stopped. Frowned. "I don't remember this row not being full. She has...had... tons of books and never left blank spaces on the shelves."

"Where are the rest of the books?" Judah asked.

Cassie moved to the closet and opened it. There was a box on the top shelf that she pulled down and then unpacked on the desk, in neat stacks. The overflow books seemed to be mostly literature books, classics and a couple of anthologies. She took out three books and fit them into the empty space on the shelf.

"That's better," she said quietly, then frowned at the shelf. "Still...what if..." She met Jake's eyes like she was looking for something, though he didn't know what. He nodded his chin down slightly in encouragement. She looked at Judah. "What if they took some of the books?" She winced. "I know that must sound ridiculous."

"Stranger things have happened. You're here because I trust your eyes, Cassie. I've heard you knew your aunt better than anyone and that means something. If something strikes you as off, even if you can't articulate why, it's worth looking into."

"I'm sure she wouldn't have left her shelves like that, with some books off. She was pretty particular about this room, actually. I wasn't allowed to borrow her books

without permission, like it was her own kind of library."
Cassie wore a slight smile. "She used to keep a list where
I could sign books out, after she'd given me her permission to read them. I didn't read every book she had, but
I read this list enough times to remember most of the
titles." She opened the top desk drawer. Jake moved
closer to see. The contents were disorganized, but she
pulled out a few typed pages of paper.

"Here they are." She set them on the desk, then started
scanning the pages. Stopped. Glanced at the shelves.
Looked back down.

"I know what's missing."

Jake and Judah both waited. Jake could feel the room
grow even more still as they braced themselves for whatever she was about to say.

"But it doesn't make any sense. She actually has some
valuable books in this collection."

"Cassie, which books?" Jake spoke up, hoping to keep
her focused.

"She had a few self-published books about Raven
Pass. Those are what's missing."

Books about the town?

"Let's look through the rest of the house," Judah suggested, clearly dismissing the idea that the missing books
were relevant to the investigation.

None of the rooms past the library down the hall had
been touched, which in Jake's mind gave credence to
Cassie's idea that the books had been taken intentionally. Judah seemed baffled. He was a nice enough guy
and Jake didn't get the impression he disbelieved Cassie
or anything. Just that her observations didn't jibe with
his assumptions about the case.

"When the officers tasked with the recovery come

"One Minute" Survey

You get up to **FOUR books** <u>and</u> Mystery Gifts...

Dear Reader,

Your opinions are important to us. So if you'll participate in our fast and free "One Minute" Survey, **YOU** can pick up to four wonderful books that **WE** pay for!

As a leading publisher of women's fiction, we'd love to hear from you. That's why we promise to reward you for completing our survey.

IMPORTANT: Please complete the survey and return it. We'll send your Free Books and Free Mystery Gifts right away. **And we pay for shipping and handling too!** *We pay for EVERYTHING!*

Try **Love Inspired® Romance Larger-Print** books and fall in love with inspirational romances that take you on an uplifting journey of faith, forgiveness and hope.

Try **Love Inspired® Suspense Larger-Print** books where courage and optimism unite in stories of faith and love in the face of danger.

Or TRY BOTH!

Thank you again for participating in our "One Minute" Survey. It really takes just a minute (or less) to complete the survey... and your free books and gifts will be well worth it!

Sincerely,

Pam Powers

Pam Powers
for Reader Service

"One Minute" Survey

GET YOUR FREE BOOKS AND FREE GIFTS!

✓ Complete this Survey ✓ Return this survey

▼ DETACH AND MAIL CARD TODAY!

1 Do you try to find time to read every day?
☐ YES ☐ NO

2 Do you prefer books which reflect Christian values?
☐ YES ☐ NO

3 Do you enjoy having books delivered to your home?
☐ YES ☐ NO

4 Do you find a Larger Print size easier on your eyes?
☐ YES ☐ NO

YES! I have completed the above "One Minute" Survey. Please send me my Free Books and Free Mystery Gifts (worth over $20 retail). I understand that I am under no obligation to buy anything, as explained on the back of this card.

☐ I prefer Love Inspired® Romance Larger Print 122/322 IDL GNTG
☐ I prefer Love Inspired® Suspense Larger Print 107/307 IDL GNTG
☐ I prefer BOTH 122/322 & 107/307 IDL GNTS

FIRST NAME

LAST NAME

ADDRESS

APT.#

CITY

STATE/PROV.

ZIP/POSTAL CODE

back to town, we will fingerprint the house and see if forensic evidence indicates anything," Judah said as they all walked toward the front door. "And we will call you if we need anything else."

"Okay." Cassie nodded but seemed hesitant.

Jake reached for her hand and tugged her along with him onto the front porch. "Thanks, Officer Wicks. Keep us posted if you will."

"As much as I can." Judah nodded. Jake suspected a call to Levi would probably get him further with information, but he appreciated that the other man at least seemed to understand why they cared so much.

Cassie followed him to the car and they both climbed in. When he shut the door and reached for his keys, he turned sideways enough to see that Cassie's eyes were flashing fire at him.

"Whoa, what's the matter?"

"I wasn't done talking to him and you pulled me out of there like I was yours to control." She rubbed at her hand, at the spot that he'd held. Like doing so would wipe away all evidences of physical contact that had been between them.

He took a deep breath. "I know you weren't done. I can tell."

She opened her mouth but he shook his head and kept talking. "Cassie, stop. Trust me, okay? I know you had more questions, but Judah wasn't the man to ask. He wasn't impressed with the books being missing, and I don't think he was going to listen to any more of your speculations. I, however, am happy to listen, and we're going to go pick up our son, feed him some food, and then after he goes to sleep, you and I are going to discuss it and come up with our own plan of action, okay?"

"Our own plan…" Her eyebrows were raised, the look on her face slightly wary.

"I think we should look into it. The books, I mean. You know which ones they were?"

"I memorized the three titles on the list. The ones that are missing."

"Well either your aunt hid something in one of those books, which is possible, though you'd think they'd have taken it and left the book itself—or there was something in one of the books they were interested in."

"Something worth killing over? I wondered all of that too, that's why I wanted to talk to Officer Wicks. But it doesn't make sense. Why not get the books from the library? Surely they have them."

"Did she make notes in her books?"

Cassie nodded, eyes wide.

"So there may have been notes."

He saw the question asked again in her eyes, from earlier. *Something worth killing over?*

Very possibly. They were close. Jake could feel it. Her aunt's death hadn't been random or a crime of opportunity, not if the house had been gone through like this and things taken.

And Jake was confident that he and Cassie would be able to figure things out.

Cassie couldn't remember ever being flooded with relief quite as much as right now, as her son ran to her open arms while Jake waited in the car for them.

"Did you have a good day?" she asked, bending to kiss his cheek and inhale the scent of his hair.

"It was so fun! They have a bunch of wooden swords and we fought bad guys all day."

Relief was quickly replaced by alarm and Cassie felt her eyes widen as she looked up at Officer Thomas. "Bad guys?"

"Imagined only." He shrugged. "Boys, you know?"

Especially a boy whose dad was a police officer, and a boy who had been shot at by some faceless villain the day before. Yes, it made sense to Cassie, even though she'd rather her little boy had been filled with thoughts of...she didn't know, caterpillars, or worms or something. Maybe boys were supposed to know about bad guys and things like that at six. Cassie didn't know, but yesterday still bothered her more than she could say. She should be thankful, she supposed, that he was processing his feelings well, acting the part of the hero in pretend play. The psychology classes she took in college would have said it was a good sign.

Still, her heart hurt.

Why? she asked again, about the whole situation. Again, no answers.

"Thank you for letting him stay here."

"No problem," Officer Thomas said. "He's welcome here tomorrow too."

Cassie nodded slowly. She wanted him with her, but... he'd been safe today, while she'd been at risk on more than one occasion. Either she stepped out of the investigation, even the informal one she and Jake seemed to be conducting on the side, or she trusted someone else to provide some of Will's care.

"We'll have him here about the same time. Thank you." She hoped her words conveyed all the gratefulness she felt.

Officer Thomas nodded.

Will hurried off to the car. Cassie followed him.

He talked all the way home—or rather, back to Jake's house. Jake Stone's house was not home and never would be.

"So can I?" Will asked her, clearly for the second time.

"Can you what?" Cassie tried to focus.

"Can I have a wooden sword?"

She opened her mouth to say no, a knee-jerk response she wasn't proud of but wasn't going to deny either. "Maybe so, bud. Ask me again when we're home, okay?"

Now she felt Jake's eyes on her, despite the fact that he was supposed to be driving and, you know, paying attention to the road. Cassie stared out the passenger-side window, his unasked questions boring through her like his gaze. What did he expect? That because she'd told him the truth about Will she'd just…pick up her whole life and stay here?

She did have a job. Not the perfect one, but a job. Same with their apartment. Will's school was good though, one of the best in their part of Florida, hence the reason she'd chosen the apartment in the first place.

Raven Pass offered what? Bad memories piled on top of other bad memories?

Not all bad, Cassie knew. But she didn't want to think about those right now.

Instead she went on some kind of autopilot mode and fixed Will dinner at Jake's house again. Over dinner, she asked if he remembered how she'd told him he had a dad somewhere. Jake had gone out of the room; where, Cassie didn't know.

"I remember. You said he loved me a lot but he didn't know me."

A slight embellishment on Cassie's part. She'd known Jake *would* love him, if he knew about him, and it was important to her that Will knew he had two parents who cared about him.

"Right. He didn't know you and it was my fault. I didn't want to share you."

Will frowned. "You're supposed to share."

"I know, sweetie, and I'm sorry. I'm…ready…" she was not ready, not even close, but she knew it was past time, so she kept going "…to share you with him now, okay?"

"So I can meet him?" Will's eyes widened.

"You have, baby… It's Jake."

Cassie braced herself, waited for the fallout she certainly deserved.

"Really? This is awesome! I'll bet he knows how to make wooden swords!" And Will jumped up from the table and went in search of the dad he'd just discovered.

Cassie was left alone, her stomach churning with questions about whether she'd handled this right, or could have done a better job of damage control for her past choice to leave Jake out of Will's life.

You told him? Jake mouthed in her direction when he came in a few minutes later, Will attached to his side like a koala.

Cassie nodded.

A shadow flickered across Jake's face but he nodded too.

"Can we play a game? All three of us?" Will was practically beaming, and Cassie wondered when she should finish explaining things to him. Like the part where even though he had a dad, Cassie was only planning on Will seeing him a few times a year.

How on earth was she supposed to do this?

Instead she said nothing for now, just kept running

over options and scenarios in her mind. She and Jake played a few card games with Will until it felt like they'd all settled in enough that he should be able to get some sleep. After the last hand Cassie leaned back and took a deep breath, ready to wage the war for bedtime that seemed to be happening more often the older Will got. He sometimes seemed to think that because he "wasn't sleepy" he might not have to listen to the rules about what time he was supposed to be in bed with the lights out. The past few nights had been exceptions. He'd been so exhausted that he'd conked out as soon as his head hit the pillow.

"Time for bed, Will," Jake said before Cassie got around to it and she almost stopped him. Why, because she was Will's mom? Jake was his dad.

This was much more complicated than she'd ever really thought through, even in her most anxious moments.

Instead of fighting when she had little fight left, she sat still, kissed her son on his forehead when he came over to her with arms outstretched.

"Dad is going to tuck me in." Will smiled up at him, skipped off and left Cassie behind.

With her heartbreak, regrets and an overwhelming feeling of being alone.

"You should have waited for me to be there." When he was done tucking Will in bed and came back downstairs, Jake wasted no time telling Cassie what had been on his mind. He'd been working in his study earlier, detailing some of the search notes for the last few days, when he'd been attacked by a six-year-old boy who'd excitedly declared that Jake was his dad.

He was elated Will knew and happy he didn't have to keep it a secret anymore. He hated secrets.

But she still should have waited for him. He tried to be understanding and not overreact about the entire situation, but the frustration was all building over this one issue. He could feel it, identify it logically, and still it was hard to deal with.

"Couldn't you have let me be part of that one thing, Cassie? I've missed everything. And you had the chance to share this with me because I was right here in the same house and you still couldn't do it?"

The hurt flickering in her eyes wasn't lost on him.

But what was he supposed to do?

God, how are we ever supposed to work this out?

"I'm sorry." Her voice was soft, but something in her tone made him meet her eyes. She wasn't self-abasing or being manipulative with her apology to elicit sympathy. She was really just that sorry.

Jake nodded. "Thanks." Focusing on something else for now might be a better idea, he realized, and moved to sit in his favorite chair. Probably he should have sat down before having that last conversation at all. Two people sitting always made for more equal ground in discussions, whereas one standing made it feel unbalanced from the get-go.

"So about those books," he started.

Were those tears she was blinking back? He thought they might be, but didn't know if they were for her aunt or the way they'd both handled things with Will.

Maybe both.

"What about them?"

"Do you think the library has them?" Jake couldn't say he'd ever searched the library for books about the town. He'd been born in Anchorage and then brought back to his parents' home in Raven Pass at just a couple of days old, so town history was something he'd assumed he knew.

If someone was stealing books for information and potentially killing over it, he suspected he didn't know everything there was to know about the town.

"I would think so." Cassie shrugged. "Which means stealing my aunt's was worthless unless she *had* written things down in them."

"Did your aunt know any town secrets?"

Jake was mostly joking, but Cassie looked lost in thought.

"Cassie?" He called her name, but she still didn't respond. He waited.

"I would have said no." She shook her head. "But… I don't know… She was so strange about that office, Jake. Why *did* she make me write down books I checked out like a real library? Was she really that obsessive? Or did she not want me to read certain books?"

"You never read the ones about Raven Pass?"

"No."

"Do you know anyone who did, or anyone she might have shared them with?"

"No. She kept them to herself, as far as I know."

Jake was out of questions for now. "We need to go to the library and check out those books."

"Tomorrow after we drop Will off?" she asked, so casually that it felt as if they'd always been like this, a real couple, discussing their kid.

Of course they were a real couple doing just that. Only he'd missed six years of these types of discussions.

"Sounds good."

She caught his eyes, whether on purpose or not, he wasn't sure. It was like there was something she wanted to say but she was hesitating.

"Cassie…" He trailed off, memories of six years ago, of the kiss today, of the way he'd tried to tell her they were just friends all swirled together.

Along with guilt. Because surely she'd left for a reason. He'd tried to tell himself for years that if he'd done anything wrong, he would have fixed it if she'd asked, but was it true? Or had he driven her away somehow?

They'd had plans. Dreams. They'd finished high school and had been accepted to a college in Washington, but they'd both decided to do one year of general education courses in Anchorage first. They'd been halfway through that year when they got engaged. They'd just finished it when she left.

"What else?" Jake asked.

"What else, what? About the books?" Her expression said she knew what he meant, but that she was still afraid to go down this road again. It hurt to relive—he got that. But maybe if he understood, they'd finally have some kind of closure and could figure out how to work well together parenting Will, from however far apart they lived.

"About when you left. Please tell me why. The whole truth."

She opened her mouth to talk when Jake heard the first noise that sounded out of place. Then he heard a creak, a scratch against the siding of the house. Something he wouldn't have noticed before this week, but that now sent alarm bells off in his head.

"Get upstairs."

Cassie was already on her way. A feeling of déjà vu swept over him.

Last time Jake had sent her up there, the man had come inside hunting them, or at least Cassie, when Jake was outside trying to find him. And Jake was putting them all in play the same way. The guy after her was smart, Jake realized, as he moved to a window to see if he could see anything outside. He saw nothing out of place, just dim, hazy midnight sun. The culprit probably expected his noises to draw Jake outside, away from Cassie's side, as they had before.

This time he might get to Cassie. And Jake wasn't going to let that happen. He grabbed his cell phone off the side table by the chair and took the stairs two at a time. Barely winded because adrenaline was coursing through his veins, he made it upstairs just as Cassie was starting to shut the door.

"I'm coming with you." He kept his voice low but saw Will stir on the bed anyway, a shadow in the dim room. His blackout curtains darkened it well. He walked into the room, picked Will up.

"Get his pillows," he told Cassie and opened the closet door with his foot.

"What are you doing?" she whispered after she'd slid the pillow into the closet where Jake was heading with Will and he'd settled their son down on the floor in the back corner. He was glad he kept this closet fairly empty.

"Keeping us safe," he answered as he dialed the police department and described the situation. Five minutes, they told him, and they'd be there.

Jake hoped the guy hung around for five minutes. Then maybe this could all be over, and they could get on with their lives. His breath caught in his throat when he realized that once the danger passed, Cassie would leave again. But at least she'd be safe. Maybe even happy. And that was what Jake wanted.

"Shouldn't you go out there?"

"And let them get to you? No. I'm staying here."

Jake felt his heart pounding in his chest. From fear? Or proximity to the only woman he'd ever loved? Cassie leaned closer and he felt the pace of it quicken even more. That answered that question.

"I'm scared, Jake."

Her voice was low, quavering. He didn't think she'd admitted that this entire time, though she'd already been in enough situations where it would have been appropriate to admit that it was the truth. Without thinking, he reached for her and tugged her close, right up against him in the darkness.

"It's okay. The police will be here any minute."

"That's not what I mean."

Jake frowned, loosed his arms a little, but when she snuggled closer—something he wouldn't have thought possible—he tightened them again. *God, please help me understand why she feels so good in my arms if she's not supposed to be here. Am I supposed to be getting over her? Or asking for another chance?*

He swallowed hard. "What are you scared of?"

"This."

Jake listened hard for sounds outside the closet that would mean they were in trouble. He heard nothing. Though he felt plenty, like he was in trouble in here.

He wanted to ask her what she meant by *this* but he knew full well what she meant. And she had to know it too.

"We aren't just friends, Jake," she said, her voice bolder

than he could ever remember hearing it. Not brazen though. Just confident. Irresistibly so.

And she was right. They weren't just friends.

That didn't mean being anything more made sense.

But he couldn't tell her she was wrong.

All he could do was keep listening for trouble. Keep breathing.

And keep trying not to kiss her again even though it was all he wanted to do right now. Jake closed his eyes and swallowed hard, temptation filling him.

If there was any hope of them being together again one day, he wanted things to be different this time. He wanted to honor Cassie and show her how special she was. That meant kisses were going to be a little more limited. Given out carefully.

And not in dark closets.

"I don't think I ever stopped loving you, Jake."

The words he'd always wondered about hit him with the velocity of an unexpected freight train.

His phone rang. It was Levi's cell.

"You're here?" he asked by way of greeting.

"Yes. We saw a truck driving away in front of your house, but no one else here. No sign of anything."

"I'll come downstairs and talk to you." Jake stood and Cassie looked at him questioningly.

"That's Levi Wicks. They don't see anyone out there but I want to check it all out for myself before I go to bed."

"I'll come with you." She stood too and there they were, achingly close again.

"You need to stay inside in case Will needs you, okay?" Or in case of a sniper who'd positioned himself somewhere outside and was lying in wait. Either reason was solid.

"Okay, I'll stay in the living room downstairs," she said as she followed him out of the closet. He watched her look back at Will and hesitate.

"Leave him there for now. It's safer."

Cassie nodded.

Jake talked to the officers downstairs, but it was as Levi had said. There was no sign of attempted entry, and there were no suspects on the premises. They hadn't recognized the truck, and it had been too dark to get a license number.

He felt cheated. Like they'd come so close to stopping the man or men behind this and then only been taunted. And left to recover from the adrenaline crash that came with wondering if this was it—the end of being hunted one way or the other.

When the police drove away, he came back inside and told Cassie what he'd learned, which was fairly close to nothing, but she seemed to appreciate knowing anyway.

After about a minute of silence, letting the news soak in, Cassie stood. "I guess I'll go try to get some sleep." She seemed hesitant and he suspected she might want to pick up the conversation where they'd left off, but he couldn't handle any more tonight. He needed a break. So he just nodded and watched her walk back up the stairs.

"Cassie?" He couldn't stop himself. She paused on the fourth step from the bottom.

"About earlier?"

She waited.

"I'm sure I never stopped loving you."

TEN

Despite the weight of so many events the day before, or maybe because of them, Cassie slept better than she had in ages. If there had been any more suspicious noises throughout the rest of the night, she hadn't heard them. She stretched, blinking her eyes to try to get some moisture back into them. Then she glanced at the clock.

Past nine o'clock. The library was open by now and they needed to see those books. Cassie fumbled her way out of the covers she'd heaped on top of herself and carried a pile of clean clothes to the bathroom where she took the fastest shower she could and then braided her hair. She never did her hair this way in Florida, but it seemed natural here just to braid it wet and have it out of the way, hanging over her shoulder and down in front on one side just like it had when she was in high school and too busy adventuring to worry too much about her looks.

Of course, Jake had always thought she was beautiful. She'd never doubted that. He'd been good to her, good for her.

And he still loved her. What was she supposed to do with that information? It didn't change the fact that she'd left and didn't deserve him. And it certainly didn't erase all the obstacles.

What Cassie couldn't decide was if it made it harder or easier.

"Wake up, sweetie." She shook Will gently until he finally blinked his own eyes open.

"It's morning already? I barely slept."

Cassie laughed, thinking of the way they'd carried him into the closet, and then how she'd moved him out after she'd come back upstairs for the last time, sure that danger had passed, at least for the moment, and not wanting Will to wake up in the closet and ask questions. By moving him, she'd effectively kept him from knowing that anything strange had happened last night, and after the trauma he'd endured with the gunshots the day before, she was happy with that.

"It's morning and you get to go back to the house with the swords." She kept her voice light, and sure enough, that was all it took to launch Will from bed and send him into a flurry of tooth brushing and clothes changing.

By the time they got downstairs, Jake was dressed too, sitting in a chair, drinking his coffee.

"You guys all ready?" He smiled and Cassie thought she read in his look a hint of teasing at how late she'd slept. Well, let him tease her. She felt amazing and after the last few days she didn't even feel bad. She'd needed that extra rest.

"Ready." Cassie nodded to confirm.

"Breakfast?"

She patted the small backpack she'd slung over her shoulder. "I packed granola bars."

"Those are not breakfast." He made a face and walked to the kitchen, pulled two plates out of the oven and handed one to each of them. "I made waffles and kept them warm for when you woke up."

"You *made* these?" Cassie confirmed as she set her backpack down to take the plate.

He shrugged. "I've had to eat all these years, you know. How did you think I did that without learning how to cook?" He laughed, and Cassie and Will sat down at the counter on a couple of stools. Cassie guessed the library would still be there in five minutes, but it had been a long time since anyone had made breakfast for her. She certainly wasn't going to let that go to waste.

When breakfast was finished, they piled into the car and drove to Officer Thomas's house to drop Will off. When Cassie moved to get out of the car to update the officer on the other possible attempted attack last night, Jake held out a hand to stop her. "I've got it, okay?"

His face was so hopeful, like he wanted to have this chance to be involved in Will's life, be the one to drop him off, that Cassie couldn't say no. She nodded. "Okay."

She hugged and kissed Will, and he made a face about the kiss on his cheek like he always did. Then he and Jake were off and she sat waiting for a few minutes until Jake returned.

"Everything okay?"

"He's got it under control." Jake let out a breath. "It's a huge relief to have him out of danger during the day."

It was, Cassie had to admit, if only to herself.

They drove to the library and were there within minutes, one of the perks of a small town. Cassie didn't bring up anything about their conversation the night before. Despite what he'd said, she still felt some kind of hesitation in Jake. There was something keeping them from a second chance, but she didn't know what it was and wasn't sure he did either. Besides, they had too much to think about right now, trying to figure out why her aunt had been killed.

And by whom.

They parked in front of the library, a building with a gorgeous mural of Fourteen-Mile River painted on the side of it. That was one thing Cassie had missed in Florida. The municipal building artwork in Alaska was special.

Had she admitted to herself how much she loved it here and how much she missed it? Cassie didn't think so.

"Don't tell anyone why we're looking," Jake said to her, his voice low as he held the glass door for her at the library's entrance. She nodded, but wouldn't have thought of it if Jake hadn't told her. She'd always felt safe in libraries, maybe because her aunt had taken her so much when she was a kid and encouraged her to read.

Still, danger reached every corner of Raven Pass she'd been in so far. Cassie needed to remember not to let her guard down, and to assume that the threat could find her anywhere.

"Hello." The librarian, Mrs. Carpenter, had to be at least as old as the building itself. At least that's how she seemed to Cassie, because she couldn't remember a time without the woman working there. In reality, she was probably only a few years older than Cassie's aunt was…had been… But her hair had gone white early, so when Cassie was younger, she'd always assumed she was ancient.

"Hi, Mrs. Carpenter." Cassie smiled.

Jake frowned at her. Apparently he'd not only meant to keep quiet about what they were looking for, but he would have preferred for them to slip in unnoticed entirely.

Oops.

"Anything I can help you with today, dear?" she asked, then her eyes behind her glasses clouded over. "I'm sorry to hear about your aunt."

"Thanks." Cassie darted a glance at Jake. He still wasn't looking much friendlier. "And no, we don't need help," Cassie said and watched Jake's face relax as she said so.

"All right, just let me know." Mrs. Carpenter went back to her work on the computer.

Cassie walked with Jake to the back of the library, where the books about the town were. She pulled the slip of paper from her pocket that she'd written the books' names on last evening to assure herself that she wouldn't forget them.

They searched the shelves. The library had all three books.

Finally something was going their way.

Jake pulled the books from the shelf and nodded to one of the study tables nearby. It sat under a window, with a view of Fireweed Mountain. Cassie followed him over there and they sat, the books stacked between them on the table. Something in Cassie's stomach felt heavy. These books, while not the exact copies that had been stolen, somehow felt like one of the links she had left to her aunt.

And maybe the reason for her death? Cassie didn't know how, but it made sense. Why else would someone have taken them?

But what kind of notes could have been worth killing someone for? And why would the killer have gone after her too?

"I wish you hadn't said hi to the librarian," Jake whispered.

"Mrs. Carpenter? Why?" Cassie frowned. "I didn't tell her why we were here."

"Yeah, but librarians talk, you know? When was the last time you were in here?"

Cassie couldn't answer. She didn't even remember.

"I don't want her to notice our presence and tell someone about it. We have no idea who it is we're trying to protect you from, and we can't afford her talking to the wrong person."

It made sense to Cassie.

"Sorry. I'll be sneakier."

Jake raised his eyebrows. "It would be hard not to be sneakier than that."

Cassie made a face, then looked at the stack of books again. Reached for one of them.

She opened the first book. It didn't tell her too much she hadn't heard. Raven Pass had been founded over one hundred years ago by miners, but they hadn't lasted long in the Alaskan climate and their settlement had come to ruin. Settlers tried again in the 1930s, when another gold rush farther north inspired people to try in many different places. One of them found gold then, or so the legend went. But no one knew for sure because the gold had disappeared around the time of a grisly double murder.

Cassie had forgotten, somehow, the legend of the Raven Pass gold. Odd, because she could remember people talking about it, especially the elementary school–aged kids, around Halloween. The whole town had been fascinated by it. Eventually talk had died down some, but it was still one of those things everyone in Raven Pass knew about, just by virtue of being from there.

Jake was looking through another one of the books, but he stopped reading and looked at her. "Your aunt didn't know about the gold, did she?"

"The legend?" Cassie whispered back, conscious to keep her voice at a library-appropriate level, and of the fact that someone could be listening. "Of course she did. All of us do."

He shook his head. "That's not what I mean. Did she know more about it?"

She'd barely talked to Cassie about it. That didn't really speak to someone who had extra information about the subject.

Unless it did. Unless she'd been keeping something from Cassie. Was it easier not to talk about the subject at all than to try to be selective about what information she shared?

Which fit with the aunt she'd known. Cassie didn't know what to say, didn't know what to think.

Chills went down her backbone the more she thought about it, and the idea of sitting in front of the window was awkward.

"Can we leave?" she asked Jake, swallowing hard. "I feel…weird."

Like someone was watching her.

He nodded. "Let's make copies of the pages about the treasure and the rumors."

"Out of the whole book, you're that sure it's what it has to do with?"

"What else about Raven Pass could lead to someone being willing to commit murder? The gold and the legend make sense."

Cassie knew he was right, but it didn't make sense at all. Not really. Not with everything she remembered about her aunt. She shivered again and moved away from the window.

Somehow it felt like someone was out there. And whether Cassie was being paranoid or not, she couldn't shake the feeling, couldn't stop her skin from crawling.

Would she ever feel safe again?

Making copies didn't take long and Jake was able to do it without asking for help. He was relieved by that. He didn't want the older woman talking about why they'd been there researching.

As it was, no one would ever know. He finished making copies of the last book, only the sections about the Raven Pass gold and the legend that surrounded it, and then returned the books to the shelf. Cassie followed along behind him, not saying much, but clearly not wanting to be alone.

"Are you okay?" he finally asked her as he pulled the finished copies out of the machine.

She shook her head. "No." Her voice was even quieter than the library called for. "I feel weird. Like when I'm near a window, someone's watching me."

"Which window?" he asked, not willing to take chances.

She nodded her head toward where they'd been sitting earlier. Jake walked over to it, careful to keep Cassie out of the line of vision from anyone outside.

But he didn't see anything out of place. Just the town itself, and the mountains on one side. This was the back of the building. The car was out front.

"I don't feel it anymore," she mumbled, then shrugged. "Maybe I am just being overly anxious."

Jake wasn't inclined to think so. Cassie wasn't the kind of woman who was naturally suspicious and concerned. If she'd felt like someone was watching her, there was a decent chance someone had been. Then why not now?

He wanted to get her back home. They could look at this information there, and while he had no illusions that his house was bulletproof either figuratively or literally, it was his home turf and therefore easier to defend and to keep Cassie safe in.

"Ready to leave?" He tried to keep his voice casual, but it did nothing to ease the tension he could see in her jaw.

"Yes, please."

They walked to the front of the library together.

"Have a good day," the librarian called. So much for sneaking out unnoticed. The woman saw everything.

Jake didn't want Cassie outside for long unprotected, even though he was pretty sure that now *he* was the one being paranoid, so he unlocked his vehicle from the entryway of the building.

"Don't waste time getting in the car, okay?"

Cassie nodded. "Okay."

For a crazy second, Jake thought maybe he felt it too, the sensation of being watched, but it was the tension overwhelming him. He wasn't the one in danger, Cassie was.

He didn't hear the concussive blast of the rifle shot until it had already kicked up part of the sidewalk a couple feet from his feet.

"Car, Cassie, now!" he yelled and looked around to

try to figure out where the shots had come from. Which left him a still target, but they weren't after him.

"Jake!"

"I'm trying to find the muzzle flash."

He saw it, somewhere on the hillside just above town to the south, just before he felt a searing pain in his arm. The force made him flinch sideways and he felt himself falling.

Then he hit the sidewalk hard and his head hurt, hurt, hurt.

Until it was all black.

He was behind her, taking too long to get to shelter, when Cassie heard the second shot and then saw him fall. Cassie didn't hesitate, but ran in his direction, knowing if he wasn't unconscious, he'd yell at her for heading toward danger instead of away from it. The fact that he didn't protest, and his eyes didn't open, told her how bad it was.

Please don't let him be dead.

She hurried to his side. She could see the bullet wound, which looked like more of a graze. At least there was that slight bit of reassurance. He wasn't going to die from that wound, not unless she couldn't get him out of the line of fire. She tugged at him but he was too heavy. She looked behind her, toward where the shot had come from.

Nothing. No hint of movement. Wasn't she the one in danger? She could be in their sights right now, kneeling on the hard concrete sidewalk that was digging through the knee of her pants. Cassie could imagine the scene. She was vulnerable, no question.

So why wasn't anyone shooting?

"Jake, you have to wake up." She shook him.

Still nothing.

"Jake. Now!" She raised the volume of her voice as she felt frustration building in her. Not toward Jake, he couldn't help it, but at the entire situation. Doubt clouding her mind, she reached for his wrist and felt for a pulse on the off chance she was wrong, and something had been fatal. The fall, maybe. Her own heart pounded as she waited for her fingers to feel the reassuring thump of his heart rate.

There it was. He was alive and breathing, she now saw when she looked at his chest. All of that was good news. He was just very, very unconscious.

Movement out of the corner of her eye caught Cassie's attention. There, coming from the side of the library, one hundred feet away, maybe, someone was heading slowly in her direction.

She opened her mouth to ask for help, human instinct overriding her caution. Until her brain finally registered that the man coming toward her was dressed entirely in black and had some kind of firearm strapped to his waist.

Not help. Someone she needed to run from.

Cassie glanced back at the car, right there, so close but doing her no good. She wondered if the librarian had heard the shot, but even if she had, here in Alaska she might just figure it was a hunter too close to town. Cassie could leave Jake, which is what she knew he would want, but she wouldn't. Not now. She'd done it once and paid for it every day since. This time, she wasn't going to make the same mistakes.

"I. Am. Not. Leaving. You!" She punctuated each word, gritted out through her clenched teeth, with a tug on Jake's shirtsleeve. On the last Jake's lashes fluttered. Then his eyes went wide.

"Hurry!" she yelled at him and he stood, slowly, but enough that she was able to pull him toward the passenger side of the car. She climbed in the driver's seat, took the keys he offered and floored it out of the space just as the man who'd been coming closer started running at her. Cassie exhaled deeply, then startled as she realized there had been another man she hadn't seen. He was dressed the same way, all black, nothing identifying about his features, running for the front of the car.

"Don't stop," Jake ordered.

Cassie kept driving but felt herself tensing as the figure moved to the center of the road. "I can't hit him."

"He'll move. Go, Cassie!"

She hit the gas. The man dove out of the way at the sound of the engine revving and relief flooded her. She drove without saying a thing for at least the next sixty seconds and then finally managed to put a thought into word form. "Are you okay?" Not wanting to take her eyes off the road, but needing to see for herself that he was really awake, alive and sitting next to her, Cassie glanced in Jake's direction quickly.

Her own heart jumped, skittered in her chest. Adrenaline, surely. Not a reaction to Jake.

Everything in her wanted to go straight to Will and pick him up, but even though a glance in the rearview mirror showed no one following them, Cassie wasn't taking any chances.

The first couple of attacks in broad daylight had been easy to explain away, at least for Cassie. First, she'd been alone during hours that most people weren't on the streets. Next, they'd been in the woods. No witnesses there except for the other people in the group.

But attacking outside the library? Shooting onto the actual sidewalks of Raven Pass? Cassie couldn't remember this kind of attempted violence in town ever. Not at any time during her childhood. She supposed at some point years before that a double murder would have had to have taken place in order for the whole Raven Pass treasure legend to be true, but even that was rumored to have happened in the mountains outside of town.

She wasn't safe here. Cassie pressed her foot down a little harder on the gas.

She shouldn't have come here. She pressed harder.

"Cassie, you've got to slow down."

His voice was calm. Steady but firm, and she let her foot off the gas immediately. "I'm sorry. I just can't..." She trailed off. Her voice was wavering, and her hands were tight on the steering wheel. Being in this kind of danger wasn't something she was used to.

"Drive us back to my house, okay?"

She had been driving with no destination in mind, but she was close to the edge of town. Cassie suspected she was subconsciously heading for Anchorage, though of course leaving town wouldn't solve any problems and she'd never leave without Will anyway.

For that matter...would she leave again ever? What was waiting for her in Florida?

Emotions still running high, she stole another glance at Jake.

"We should get you to a doctor," she said. His face looked pale, and she could tell he was hurting.

"I'm fine. Between the two of us, we can clean the wound and patch me up."

"Jake..."

"You're a nurse, right? I'm an EMT. Head home." His voice was strained, and she didn't want to upset him, so she did as he asked.

Maybe it was okay to admit that she cared about him still. Almost losing him today had made that hard to deny.

He caught her looking this time, and looked back at her. She turned her eyes back to the road immediately.

"So someone knew we were at the library..." Jake trailed off. "Did they know what we looked at? Or just that we were there? No one saw the books we looked at, not even the librarian."

"Are you thinking she let someone know that we were there? Like on purpose?" Cassie couldn't picture the old librarian being involved with any of the people who wanted her dead.

"No, but I heard the door open and close a few times while we were in there and saw some other people in the library."

"Of course, it's the library and it's morning. I would imagine that's one of their busier times." Cassie pulled into Jake's driveway, finally, and let out a deep breath when she had put the car in Park.

"My point is that she saw us come in and easily could have made a comment to someone that we were there, and they could have guessed what we were looking at."

"Like a coincidence thing? You think someone came in at the same time and passed the information along to whoever is after me." She frowned as she said the words. Were they even after her? It was starting to seem like they were after Jake.

"It could be that. I was thinking more like someone

could have been following us and watched us from a distance in the library."

Cassie shivered, remembering how she felt someone had been watching them.

"Are we going inside to continue this conversation in the house? Personally I'm partial to the house as it has water and I'm extremely thirsty, and there are some bandages in there. I'd prefer not to bleed all over my car."

Cassie felt exposed on the walk from the car into the house—Jake's garage was too full of tools and other equipment to park inside it—and right now Cassie wished she could tease him about it instead of dealing with this serious situation.

Once they were inside, she wanted to clean his wound and bandage him, but he insisted on stopping in the kitchen for water first. "Someone watching from inside the library, like you said, someone who maybe followed us there and came in afterward, could explain how I felt like I was being watched."

Jake seemed to be considering the idea, as he leaned against the counter and took another long sip from his glass. "You thought it was coming from outside though. It could just as easily have been whoever shot at us."

"True." Cassie had to concede the point. "But I'm also not used to pinpointing where someone might be watching me from. I just know when I have a general creepy feeling come over me, you know?"

That seemed to make sense to Jake.

"Either way, there's a small chance today was purely a target of opportunity, but it seems like a strange place for an attack if it was."

"It's much more likely we were attacked because we're getting closer," Cassie said, lowering her voice some even though they were the only two people in the house.

"I agree." Jake nodded. "Which means…"

"We need to turn the investigation over to the police and stay out of it?"

Jake shrugged. "I was going to say that it means we need to be extremely careful. Someone is tracking you."

ELEVEN

Cassie seemed to be thinking over his words, but told him to go into the bathroom so she could look at the bullet graze where his first aid kit was. He'd listened to her and made his way into the large guest bathroom downstairs, and she'd followed him in, but then he'd thought better of letting her touch him when his thoughts about her were already so confused, and had resisted her efforts to see it, clean it or put any kind of antiseptic lotion on it.

"Just let me see it." Cassie reached for his arm again, her tone growing more frustrated.

Jake tugged his arm away as she stretched out her hand, barely moving it away in time. He almost wished he was wearing long sleeves, but then again with the way she was taking this so seriously, she'd probably make him peel his shirt off. Not something he wanted to do in a small room alone with Cassie. Just thinking about it made him swallow hard and wish he had something else to focus on right now.

"It's fine, Cassie."

"I still think you need to go to the hospital. How are you supposed to keep me safe if you have an untreated concussion, or if this wound goes septic, hmm?" She stepped closer.

Jake stepped backward. She was cute when she was mad. He'd never tell her so, since it was far from politically correct and would only make her angrier, but it was true. He tried not to smile.

Apparently not hard enough. Her frown deepened.

"Do not laugh at me, Jake Stone." She stepped closer again.

He tried to move back, but there was nothing behind him but the bathtub. She'd blocked him into the room. Despite her warning, he laughed, and tried to deflect from the fact that he was so overwhelmed by her closeness right now that he didn't care about a stupid gunshot wound or a little head trauma. "You know, I'm a paramedic. I do know some of the same stuff you do. Concussion protocol, wound care…"

"And you're also proof of the fact that doctors or people in the medical field make the worst patients. You can't treat yourself and you know it. Now hush." She grabbed his arm, far enough away from the graze that it didn't hurt. Her hands on his arm brought all his focus there, and all he could think about were her fingers on his skin.

So he hushed. Didn't say a word.

She examined the wound first, then proceeded to clean it, apply triple antibiotic and then dress it. All things he could have done himself. And without the overload of emotions.

If she hadn't left, they could have been married by now. He'd thought it more than once before, but it kept surfacing, probably because he couldn't for the life of him figure out why they weren't. On his end, were there any real reasons not to start something again? Other than the fear of being hurt.

Fear was no way to live. He'd almost died today.

Maybe that was why when she came near, he caught his breath, was fully aware of how close their faces were with her leaning down like that, and how easy it would be to press his lips to hers and pick up where they'd left off with that kiss yesterday...

But it wasn't wise to do so. Not in this room alone, emotions high from the day. He'd determined to do better this time. So he decided to talk instead.

"About today..." he started.

Cassie shook her head. "I don't want to talk about it yet."

Her voice quavered at the end and Jake stopped speaking. She looked over at him, relief relaxing her features. "Thank you."

He nodded. Then couldn't resist. "I'm okay, Cassie. God protected me."

She snorted.

And he felt himself pull away.

"What did that mean?" he asked, wanting to stay calm. She'd said several things about God during their relationship and engagement that he'd been a little concerned about, but she hadn't grown up in church like he had. Jake had been raised in church and had trusted Jesus to save him when he was seven years old. Cassie...

At the time Jake hadn't known much about Cassie's story, faith-wise. He wasn't one to preach, but rather to lead by example. In hindsight, he wished he'd pushed a little more, asked more questions. He'd been in the dark then about her deepest beliefs, if she had any at all.

And the same was true now, he realized.

Dread settled in his stomach as all the pieces fit together. Her lack of knowledge, comments like this, the way she'd pulled away from any attempts at spiritual conversations when they'd dated before. "What, Cassie?" he asked again, needing to know now. He had years' worth of questions he feared might be getting answered right now.

Did Cassie even know Jesus? Jake wasn't judging. He didn't think doubts defined a person's faith. But the fact was…he wasn't sure she'd ever given him any reason to believe she trusted Jesus personally. She'd only been very tolerant of his faith, he now realized.

"I just don't know why you say stuff like that."

"About God protecting me?" That seemed obvious to him. He was alive. She was alive. Surely she could see how that provided some evidence of God at work, especially when one considered how many other times they'd been attacked in the last few days.

"If He's God, why doesn't He just stop it all, Jake? Why?" She'd stopped doctoring his arm and was pacing the bathroom, looking back at him now and then. Her shoulders were tense, in a defensive posture, like this was something she wasn't fully comfortable talking about.

Now that he let himself think about it, Jake remembered her asking before about how God could let bad things happen, but he'd written it off as a common struggle some Christians have.

Now he was wondering…

"Cassie, it comes down to this. Do you trust Jesus?"

She stopped. Looked straight at him. "No, Jake, I really don't."

And he didn't know what to say to that. Instead he

prayed, right there, his arm bandaged, head pounding, sitting on the closed lid of a toilet while the woman he'd wanted to marry stood in front of him telling him that they never should have planned to get married in the first place.

Why had he never realized Cassie didn't believe?

God, why did I fall so deeply in love with her if I was never supposed to have her? He'd no sooner articulated the prayer than he rejected part of its premise. He had full confidence they were supposed to be together. Or... were supposed to have been at one point?

All confidence faded.

I love her, God. But she doesn't love You.

And they had a son together. But she wasn't a believer.

What did he do with that?

"Cassie." Jake took a breath, focused on her, on the fact that there was a real person in front of him, one he loved very much, who didn't understand how much the God who created the world loved *her* personally. "I don't want to fight with you, but I promise, God can handle your anger, okay? He's real and He gets what we are feeling better than we do. You can ask Him all this stuff."

"Even if I'm not sure I believe in Him?" Her face was defiant, but he saw in her eyes a flicker of hope he chose to cling to.

"Talk to Him, Cassie. And think about this week, okay?"

"My aunt was killed. Not died in her sleep or anything like that, killed. Homicide. You know the coroner is going to confirm that. That's what happened this week."

"And even though we've been shot at multiple times, we are okay. Will is okay. Even the fact that you left before could have saved your life—what if you and Will had been with your aunt the day she was taken? Look at the other side here and maybe you'll see God at work, Cassie."

"I may not." She said it like a warning. But she didn't argue, and Jake thought that was positive.

"Just try, okay?"

She nodded and then moved back to him. "How is your head? Any double vision?"

He let her keep nursing him for now, even while his heart pounded along with the churning in his stomach. He still loved her. But he couldn't let himself think past being her friend for now, not when she didn't believe like he did. Even if the Bible didn't say not to marry an unbeliever, he'd known too many people who had divorced over faith issues. When he did get married, he wanted it to be forever.

But he also wanted it to be with Cassie.

God, help me. And help her believe.

Cassie turned over in the bed again and pushed the button on her cell phone to see the time. 2:28 a.m. At this rate, she might not sleep at all tonight, if she didn't fall asleep soon.

Jake's words from earlier, about God's protection, kept rolling through her mind. It was crazy how much shifting her perspective, to tentatively wondering if his explanation could be right, made her see things differently.

Could it be true that God had protected them?

Yes, she admitted finally as she turned over another time, back to the side where she'd started just now.

But still, why let the bad things happen in the first

place? That was a question she couldn't seem to answer. Would reading the Bible help, or would it just push her further away?

It was important to Jake that she believed. They'd been in some kind of dance all day long, since that kiss. Toward each other, then away. Together. Away. Jake was pulling away again and she knew it was because of the faith issue. Cassie also knew from all the times she'd spent listening to Jake's pastor preach in church during high school that she couldn't make decisions about her own relationship with God—like if she wanted to have one—based on someone else. It was a personal thing. That much she understood.

But she didn't understand God. And she wanted to.

But maybe she wasn't supposed to.

Her head was starting to hurt, whether in sympathy to Jake's injury or from all the thinking, or more likely exhaustion, she wasn't sure. Cassie rubbed her forehead and rolled to her stomach, burying her face in the pillow.

Okay, God, if You're real, I'll give You a chance to show me, okay? Just make it clear. Like maybe help us with this case. And help me get to sleep.

Cassie sank deeper into the pillow and felt herself drifting off.

She woke up to crying, but slowly, like her body had been so deep into sleep it had to shake off several layers of mental blankets to even make it to this dazed, half-awake state.

There was a shadow at the foot of the bed holding Will, who was crying. She tensed but instantly relaxed when she realized it was Jake. Holding their son.

Cassie blinked her eyes to wake up, to get used to the darkness, and to try to reconcile what she was seeing.

She wanted to be with this man forever. Why did she keep trying to deny that? The way he held Will so carefully amazed her. Still, it wasn't helping Will who looked to be having one of his rare, but occasional, night terrors.

"He won't stop crying." Jake's voice was heartbroken and puzzled. "Does he want you?"

"Sometimes he can't wake up. It's like his mind gets stuck." Cassie reached for him and sat him up. "Will, buddy? Can you hear me?"

It took a few seconds but he eventually nodded.

"Okay, it's time to go to sleep now."

He started to cry again. Cassie wanted to cry too. She was exhausted, and when she was awake, she was thinking about her aunt and the fact that she'd never get to see her again. Memories of her aunt brought back remembrances of nights like these. It had been her aunt who'd woken up with her, who'd tucked her in at night. Her dad had done what he could but he'd been grieving her mom's abandonment and he'd been so busy with work. Much of her comfort as a kid had come from her aunt.

"Want me to tell you a story?" she asked as she thought about Aunt Mabel. She'd told her the same bedtime story nearly every night. It had been years since she'd heard it, and she'd never thought before to tell it to Will, but being up here in Alaska made her nostalgic. And it was a tiny piece of her aunt she could hold onto. "Listen, my sweetheart, to this tale. For from it, you will learn how to do the right thing, and from the truth, never to turn."

The familiar opening slipped off her lips like she'd told it a thousand times instead of just listened to it. Memory was a funny thing. Cassie snuggled her son closer and continued.

"Once upon a time there was a princess who was as kind as she was beautiful. Her hair was golden, and the men of the kingdom were enchanted with her. One night, while she was sleeping in her castle at the base of a mountain, a man stole her away to his mountain cave. The man who had planned to marry the princess was brokenhearted and determined to find her. He pushed through crowds of trees and devil's club to trace the steps her captors had taken. He climbed mountains."

Will smiled a little. "I climbed a mountain."

"You did," Cassie agreed. "Part of one, anyway. Back to the story, okay? Ah yes, the prince. So he climbed mountains. He ignored the promise of other thrones if he'd abandon his quest and followed straight ahead instead. He was not stopped by rivers, and he even pursued, like true north, his princess, into the heart of darkness where she was kept. He navigated the maze to the dungeon. Left, right, left, left, and there she was alone and cold. He gathered her in his arms and kissed her, but he didn't just stay there. He took her back to the town, where the people had loved her, and they were married there."

"I saw a throne once," Will mumbled as Cassie settled him back down onto his pillow, since he'd looked to her like he was sleeping. And maybe he was, he certainly wasn't making much sense.

"Okay, sweetheart." It was better to agree with him when he was like this.

"When we were hiking. There was a throne on the rock. We turned there and walked a *looooooong* way…" His voice trailed off and Cassie smiled at him. Then her smile fell.

She looked at Jake.

They had turned, abandoned a trail at a rock that, according to Will, had looked like a throne. They hadn't continued straight ahead.

Shivers crawled down her arms, then back up again. "You don't think…"

He nodded slowly. "Your aunt knew where the Raven Pass treasure was."

Cassie whispered back. "And she told me how to find it."

TWELVE

Jake led them to the room where they'd talked the other night and Cassie had been so sure there wasn't any kind of second chance for them. She wasn't sure how she felt now. Sometimes she was positive Jake still cared, and at other times she knew she'd destroyed what they had beyond repair years ago.

Right now she didn't know what she thought. The look on his face… Her stomach jumped if she paid too much attention. But he sat in a chair after she'd taken the couch, which seemed to imply he didn't want to be that close to her.

Stop analyzing.

Cassie started talking so she'd stop thinking and over-thinking. "Thanks for calming him down before I woke up, or trying anyway." She offered him a smile as she sat. "It was so weird seeing someone else hold him and take care of him… I missed that, raising him alone. And I'm sor—"

He cut her off before she could apologize again. "You've already told me you're sorry. It doesn't change the past, okay? Just let it go. I'm trying to."

Was it that easy for him? Because it wasn't for Cassie.

Her shoulders sagged as she attempted once again to take the grace he was offering her. It didn't seem real, the way he was willing to forgive her for it and move on. But then again, that's what his church taught, and what Jake said that the Bible taught too. Jake took his faith seriously, so maybe Cassie should understand his behavior.

It was strange to Cassie that Jake should have been so surprised by her own lack of faith. She'd never meant to give him the impression while they were dating and then engaged that she agreed with him. But she was respectful and had assumed that meant something to him. Still, he'd acted strange since she'd told him that no, she didn't trust God like he did. Or at all, for that matter.

She hadn't read enough of the Bible to know if there was a reason that the faith aspect could be a deal breaker for him, but it was bothering him to some degree.

"So tomorrow..." Cassie decided it was better to stick with a neutral subject, and this was the only one they had. The rest of the possible topics of conversation were littered with unseen landmines.

"We need to get back to the trailhead and see if we can find the treasure."

"For real, Jake, isn't it time we involve the police? Especially because I'm starting to wonder if you were the target of the gunshots all along. Maybe they'd planned..." She stumbled. "...to kill you and then take me like they did my aunt. To try to make me help them find the treasure. They must assume I know where it is."

He shook his head. "We still have no proof. We only have a guess. And you saw how Judah looked at us last night. I may send a text to Levi, just as a courtesy to a friend, but the department as a whole is not impressed with our working theory. Besides, the fewer people who

know, the safer you might be. Remember the library—
someone must have seen you there, tipped someone off."

Cassie knew he was right. She'd seen the look on Officer Judah Wicks's face when she mentioned her idea.
He didn't seem to be a man given to guesses or hunches;
she could tell from the brief dealings she'd had with him.
Best-case scenario would be they turned over their idea
to the police, and the authorities ran with it, catching
their culprit. Worst-case? Their information stirred up
more trouble, more risk. Possibly for nothing, if their
theory wasn't correct.

It was better not to say anything. After all, nothing
they were doing was illegal or even unethical. Unwise?
Possibly. But Cassie had grown desperate to try to find
whoever killed her aunt whatever way she was able. Her
only hesitation was Will's safety, but the situation they
had worked out right now with him staying with that
other family was going well.

Of course, the father, who was a police officer and the
reason Cassie felt comfortable with the deal, had to go
back to work in two days. They had tomorrow, the next
day, and then that option would be taken from them and
Will would be back with Cassie. She'd be out of the investigation then, formal or informal or otherwise. She'd
lock herself up in this house with her son until someone
else solved the case if she had to, but she wouldn't expose him to any danger if she could help it.

"So…"

Cassie hadn't realized until just then that Jake was sitting there, watching her as she thought. She had a feeling
every idea she'd considered, every emotion, must have
been displayed clearly on her face, because he looked

hesitant, like he knew she was having second thoughts. And third thoughts.

"I think you're right," she heard herself say before she was sure she was ready. "We need to go hunt some treasure tomorrow."

"Okay, so let's look at the map and mark the places we think relate to the fairy tale, shall we?"

He pulled up an internet satellite map system on the laptop he'd brought to the chair with him. Cassie could barely see it from where she was on the couch, because of the angle of the screen.

Jake glanced her way and noticed her problem. "Sorry," he said, then picked up the laptop and moved next to her. Not so close that their thighs were touching, but on the same couch anyway.

Cassie felt her breath catch ever so slightly and wished she could roll her eyes at herself without Jake noticing. What was she, sixteen with a crush?

No, this was the same man she'd had a crush on when she was that age though, which was maybe why her feelings were so strong. Jake had been her first and only love. Men had asked her out in Florida, but she'd used Will as an excuse, going on one or two first dates before giving up on the proposition entirely. She was focusing on being a single mom, she told people.

She still loved Jake. That was the truth. She'd been close last night, when she said she wasn't sure. But now she was. Fully, completely sure. She felt her shoulders relax as the tension left her body.

If they could just get past this, find the treasure, get some assurance of safety...

Then was there a chance? Jake's words had led her to believe there was, last night. But he'd not indicated anything of the sort today. Cassie believed some people who were truly in love with someone else never did get their happily-ever-after. Even if both of them loved each other. Relationships failed for a lot of reasons, or never got fully off the ground. They had enough reasons between them to ruin several relationships.

The biggest was the way she'd kept Will from him. But he insisted she didn't need to apologize anymore, so that meant it was in the past, right?

That maybe they had some kind of future?

"Do you see this line right here?" Jake motioned to the computer screen and Cassie turned her attention back to it. Yes, there in the trees, a thin line of tan seemed to go into the woods and then disappear.

"Yes."

"Part of that is where we were the other day. But judging by the directions in your story…" He frowned. "Can you say it again for me?"

"I'll do better than that. I'll write it down if you'll bring me some paper." She smiled up at him and he handed her the computer while he went to get a notebook. She studied the aerial view of the location as he did so. Strange to think that the location of the treasure could have been photographed by satellite. Of course they couldn't see the treasure or any indication of where it was, not from the altitude of the picture, but the general topography, trees, rivers were all there—it was strange to think it was there too, hidden.

So close. Still so far.

"Here you go." He handed her the notebook and sat back down, taking the computer from her.

This time he sat closer to her, and whether he'd done it on purpose or not, it was distracting her to no end.

Cassie reminded herself she was an adult and could certainly pay attention no matter whose thigh was pressed against hers.

She swallowed hard.

She could pay attention, right?

"Okay…" She took the pen Jake held out and started writing the story down as best she remembered it. Some of her aunt's word choices had varied. It wasn't like a poem that had particular lines, just a story. The only part repeated perfectly was the bit at the beginning about remembering what you heard.

"She really was trying to get me to remember," Cassie observed as she wrote those lines. "But why?"

Jake shook his head.

"I don't remember her talking about the treasure or the legend ever, which means she talked about it a lot less than the average Raven Pass citizen. Why spend every night then telling me how to find it?"

"She clearly didn't take it. She would have been too young or not even born then." Jake sounded like he was thinking aloud, but Cassie nodded because she agreed with him.

"Right. We may never know," Cassie offered, though she hoped that wasn't the case. But still, it was better to be prepared for the possibility than to be heartbroken if it turned out to be true. Bracing against unrealistic expectations was something she'd caught herself doing many times since her happily-ever-after with Jake hadn't happened. Yes, that had been her fault, but it didn't seem to matter.

"I think we will." He sounded much more confident than she felt. He continued working at the computer, pressing buttons, zooming in and surveying the land and then zooming out again. He finally printed the general area and together they highlighted the basic trail it sounded like they should take. Where directions were vague, they highlighted large chunks of Alaskan wilderness.

It could take days to thoroughly search the area, longer than that if they accounted for the time needed to look in extremely small spaces. But Cassie didn't think that would be necessary. *The heart of darkness* in the story could only be something like a cave, of which there weren't many in this part of Alaska, or possibly an old hollow stump hole, which sometimes seemed like vast holes in the ground, or a mining shaft. The entire area around Raven Pass, especially on the north side against those mountains, was known for having been active during at least one of the gold rushes. Cassie believed there were mining shafts that hadn't been explored since the time of the murders and the gold's disappearance, but she didn't know how difficult it would be to find them. Terrain could have changed, trees could have grown up. Even with the "throne" Will had noticed as a starting point, they could still have a considerable amount of trouble finding it from there.

Could her aunt have tried to show people where the treasure was and then been unable to find it? And why, after all these years, did someone know her aunt might have a clue to the treasure's location? Cassie just didn't know. She should probably stop speculating because it was starting to give her a headache.

Or that could be because it was the middle of the night and she wasn't sleeping.

"I need to go back to sleep," she finally said when fatigue had overwhelmed all of her senses.

"Sleep well."

Jake reached out to squeeze her arm and Cassie stopped. She'd been starting to stand, but his touch made her lose all motivation to leave.

"Thank you," she said in a whisper, meeting his eyes. "You didn't have to do any of this. You didn't have to try to keep me safe, or try to figure out why someone killed my aunt, but you are." She shrugged, suddenly feeling self-conscious and too vulnerable. Late nights made her feel this way. "Anyway, thanks."

"Cassie…"

She couldn't read his tone, couldn't tell from his voice what he wanted. And it was impossible to say who moved first, but one minute they were sitting side by side on the couch and she was talking, and the next she leaned into him, or he'd leaned into her, and they were kissing again, all the familiarity and magic of the past mingling with something that made her stomach flutter—hope of having a future.

Tired or not, Cassie didn't want the kiss to end. She kept her eyes closed, kept saying with her lips what she was still too afraid to say with her words. Jake said everything back to her.

And then he pulled away. Shook his head.

And she knew by the look in his eye that she had been wrong to think the words he'd said last night meant what she wanted them to. He was sure he still loved her, he said.

But that didn't mean they had a future.

She swallowed hard, brushed at invisible lint on her jeans. "I'm sorry, I don't know…"

"It wasn't just you." His voice was thick with feeling. "We can't do this, Cassie."

And somehow she thought maybe if she fought for

them this time, maybe if she didn't give up so easily, things would be different. "I won't leave again, Jake. I'll be here, like I promised last time. We can start over, but better, you know?"

She waited, but all he did was shake his head.

"I can't, Cassie."

She stared in his eyes till she saw it. The faith issue. It was a bigger deal to him than she'd anticipated, and it was something he hadn't known to be true the last time around.

Could they not get married because of that? It was *that* important to Jake? She wanted to be angry, but it was part of who he was. His commitment to doing what he felt was right was part of why she loved him; Cassie knew that. To change him would be changing him in such a fundamental way that he wouldn't even be the same person she was in love with.

He was being true to his beliefs. She admired him for it.

But it still broke her heart.

She stood. Nodded. "I understand." Another hard swallow. "Don't worry about it, okay? We can still figure this out together. I still want Will to know you. We'll be friends. Like you said, right?" She nodded again and turned to the door.

Then she brushed a tear from her eye.

She'd almost had the fairy-tale ending with Jake, and she'd been the villain in that story who stole it from herself by leaving. She should have known a second chance was too good to be true. She should never have gotten her hopes up.

Because the thing about hopes?

They hurt the worst when they come crashing down.

* * *

Jake sat in the dark for another half hour after Cassie left, trying to figure out what he could have done differently. Well, not kissed her for one, but she'd been sitting there, looking gorgeous, and he had told her the truth, he did still love her. He was every bit as in love with her as he had been years ago. But none of those feelings changed what was right, and she didn't believe the same way he did.

It shouldn't have been a deal breaker, not in his opinion, not when they had a son together. But truth was truth and it didn't change no matter what your preferences or situations or circumstances. Hadn't he been saying that for years? Here was his chance to live it.

When he'd thought out their situation from every angle, and spent some time praying too, Jake finally went back to bed. He slept lightly though. Too many things on his mind to do otherwise.

By the time he got downstairs for breakfast just after six o'clock, Cassie was already awake and scrambling eggs.

"Did you sleep okay?" he asked as he started toward the coffee maker to brew a pot only to find she'd already made enough for both of them. Jake blinked, the contrast to last night, the bad way it had ended, hurting him somewhere in his chest.

She shut off the burner she'd been using and separated the eggs onto two plates. She handed him one and then pulled bread out of a toaster, placing it on each plate before walking to the table. He followed.

"Not really." She finally answered the question as she reached for a jar of strawberry jam she must have put on the table earlier. She met his eyes and he blinked against the unflinching nature of her gaze. He didn't know what he'd expected after last night, maybe for her to be embarrassed, or upset with him, he wasn't sure. But he hadn't expected this. She seemed bolder. More confident.

One thousand times more beautiful and irresistible.

"I'm sorry about that," he said and then put jam on his own toast. Cleared his throat. "About the search today…"

"Do you want to start as soon as Will wakes up?"

He nodded.

"I can get him up if necessary. He has to be woken up for school usually."

"That…" He was about to say it wasn't necessary when he realized that if they didn't leave soon, he would just be sitting here, staring at Cassie after shattering any chance things between them could ever go back to how they used to be. He couldn't handle this level of awkward. Breakfast was hard enough. "That would be great, actually."

"Okay." She finished her breakfast without saying anything else to him and then started up the stairs.

She and Will came back down minutes later. Will had some quick breakfast, and Jake loaded them in the car only saying what needed to be said. He didn't feel much like talking this morning.

As he pulled out of the driveway, a shiver went down his spine. Things between him and Cassie were so strained that he felt even more pressure not to let anything happen to her today. If she was hurt it would crush him no matter what, but he did not want last night to be the final real conversation they'd had.

Surely he was overreacting. But none of the reassurances he tried to offer himself would stick. Because he wasn't being paranoid. Someone *was* after Cassie, they might want her dead, and he had no leads yet on who it could be. Neither did the police. He'd texted Levi enough times that his friend had finally sent him a message that said, Nothing new to tell.

None of it sat right with Jake. It had been too quiet, too easy and calm since the last attack—the gunshots outside of the library.

It made him feel like the danger was a rubber band being stretched and stretched and sometime soon...

It would snap.

THIRTEEN

Nothing improved after they dropped Will off.

"You remember we only have a couple more days before he stays with us again, right?" Cassie asked Jake, her voice completely void of any extra warmth. She wasn't rude. Just matter-of-fact and not especially... friendly.

Ironic, since that's what they'd established they were. *Friends*. Funny how much of a step back that could seem like.

"So we just need to figure out who was responsible for your aunt's death before then."

"Sure, we'll solve a decades-old legend superfast and eliminate our need for childcare." Jake didn't look at her, but he could hear the roll of her eyes.

Then she sighed. "Listen, Jake..."

He felt his shoulders tense, unsure of how this conversation was going to go. But he waited anyway.

"I'm sorry about that. It's not your fault that I...got the wrong idea, and...you know..." She shrugged. "Anyway, we're adults. We were in love once. We share a son. I can be nicer than I have been this morning and I'm sorry."

He wasn't sure what to say. And just as he opened

his mouth to do so, movement in the rearview mirror caught his eye. They'd just passed a narrow driveway and someone was turning out of it, toward them.

"You're buckled, right?" Jake double-checked with Cassie.

"Yes, why?"

His worst fears were realized when whoever was tailing him advanced. He couldn't see the driver well, but he could tell he was wearing a hat, low over his eyes. It was a white sedan, something like a Honda Accord, and its intentions were clear to Jake.

The road was narrow and wound up the mountain toward the trailhead. The mountainside itself was on the right and there was a guardrail on the left. Then it just dropped off. There was little room to maneuver if someone was driving aggressively. The car behind them qualified for that description now.

"What on earth?" Cassie's voice was breathless but not full of fear yet. She hadn't realized that whoever was tailing them was part of the group that was after her, or was the one person behind her. He wasn't sure quite how many people were involved, only that Cassie had said she'd seen more than one individual during the attack at the library.

There was only one person in the car behind them. Was his partner up ahead somewhere, or in town? If Jake knew, it could change how he drove. Should he keep going in, knowing they'd be alone in the trailhead parking lot and still needing to face the person behind them and possibly more people if others were involved and waiting somewhere, or turn into a driveway on the side of the road and try to change direction?

He wasn't completely sure either one would help.

Then the white car smashed into his bumper. They were thrown forward and back and Cassie's screams pierced his ears.

He wasn't going to be able to get away if the white car tried again. It accelerated, moved to the right edge of the road. If the car ran into him now, they'd be pushed directly against the guardrail on the left and the side of the mountain.

Jake hit the gas.

The car behind them slowed down.

"Are they gone?" Cassie twisted around in her seat, breathing hard, her eyes wide with pure fear.

"They are. Don't worry, okay?"

But she wasn't a child and she wasn't the kind of woman who would blindly accept reassurances. She knew they were still in danger and she wasn't going to act like that wasn't the case. Not even when he tried to offer comfort.

"Where did they go?" Now fear was creeping in the edges of her tone, and Jake felt it too, the sensation that something was coming, that a weight was pressing in on them.

They weren't safe. No matter how much of a relief it was that the car had gone.

The next pullout, Jake was taking it and driving back down the mountain. He could take Cassie and Will and just keep them safe in his house for as long as this lasted.

He said as much to Cassie as he kept driving up the road, which was too narrow to turn around in yet. He kept his eyes on the rearview mirror.

"You know you can't do that forever."

"It wouldn't be forever," he argued. "Surely the police will find them eventually."

Cassie shook her head. "You said yourself that they weren't looking at anything even related to why we think she was taken. Not the treasure or the legend or any of it. It could be literally years before they look there. Or they might close the case first." Her voice raised a bit in pitch, turned tight. He knew how much she'd loved her aunt and hated that she was having to deal with the lack of closure that resulted from not knowing who had killed her or being sure why it had happened.

"Still, I need to turn around." The pullout should be in the next half mile or so, at least he thought, but he eyed the next driveway on the right anyway, tempted to use it to turn around. He didn't want to be sitting still for that long, just in case the white car came at them from farther down the mountain at a high rate of speed.

"No."

He looked over at her, and blinked. That's how firm her voice had been.

"Jake, please. We are so close."

"I've got to call the car in anyway and let the police know." Was he really considering carrying out today's plan? When it was clear someone knew what they were doing?

No. He couldn't.

"Cassie..." He trailed off. He glanced her way and then back to the road again. Her expression made it clear she wasn't pleased, but he was much less concerned with her happiness than he was with her safety.

He'd just looked up at the rearview mirror to confirm no one was behind them when a car came flying at them down the mountain. This one was black, a crossover.

And it edged over the line toward him.

"Jake, watch out!" Cassie yelled.

Jake jerked the wheel hard to the right and worked to keep the car from crossing the edge of the road while avoiding the head-on hit from the other car. It happened so fast he didn't know how he was able to react at all. Maybe God's mercy.

The car still rammed them, despite his efforts. It spun Jake's vehicle almost forward, and swung it to the right. He fought with the wheel but couldn't control it, couldn't stop it from spinning.

They hit the side of the road hard, then the black SUV knocked them again.

Jake's head smacked the steering wheel before the air-bag deployed and threw him backward, and for the second time in two days he felt himself lose consciousness.

Please, God, no.

But nothing changed. Jake blacked out, aware of Cassie's yelling beside him, and completely powerless to help her.

When she woke up, Cassie felt like…gravel. Hard. Uncomfortable. All of her hurt. Cassie's eyes were dry, sandpapery. Her throat was scratchy. She swallowed. Licked her lips and swallowed again, desperate for some moisture.

She blinked, and saw that she was in the dark somewhere. And it was bumpy. She blinked some more, feeling much heavier than when she normally woke from sleep. Was it a side effect from the accident she'd been in? Or had someone drugged her? As her eyes focused, she was able to see that she was in the trunk of a car. Her hands were bound behind her by something that felt tough and plastic. Not rope, maybe something like zip ties. Her eyes weren't covered, because she could see variations in the dark and as they adjusted to the dim light, she was able to make out shapes in the trunk itself. It was fairly good-sized, she had room to stretch out. It was clean—there was nothing in there with her that she could use for a tool to escape.

Will. Was he safe? Cassie didn't know for sure but she hoped so. She was alone in the trunk and for now that encouraged her. She remembered being hit while she and Jake were driving to the trailhead to search using her directions and to see if they could find a location for the treasure. In retrospect, they never should have headed to do that alone.

How many mistakes would they make in their attempts to investigate? Come to think of it, probably no more now. Because their investigation was officially over. She'd been caught by whoever had been after her. Chills chased up her spine. Was this it, the last few minutes or hours or even seconds of her life? Cassie had no way of knowing and the thought tortured her.

God, help me.

What did she want help with? Her current situation? The mess she'd made of her relationship with Jake? Or life in general? Or her unbelief?

Can You help me believe, God? Much to her surprise that was what bothered her most. She'd thought about what Jake had said last night, when she couldn't sleep. She felt oddly pursued by a God she hadn't been sure existed. Like maybe He did want her to know Him and maybe He had been working on their behalf. But surrendering and trusting was so against her nature. When you trusted people, they let you down. Look at how her mom had let her and her dad down. How Cassie had then taken her own hurts and let Jake down, and by extension Will, who didn't know his own dad because of her fears.

God, I have really messed up. I don't know how I could be scared to trust You because clearly I'm not doing a great job without You. I believe You're real. I believe what I've heard in church over the years, that You sent Jesus to die in my place and if I trust that, I can live with You in Heaven and know You here, right now. Cassie was surprised at how many snippets came back to her from church services she'd sat in and conversations with Jake. She was surprised too at how she didn't feel like she was talking to air, or to the trunk walls, but really like she was talking to…God?

Help me believe more, God. Help me, okay? And if You can help me out of this too…that would be really good. I want to raise my son. I want to tell Jake I still love him. And more than that, I want to show him.

The car hit a pothole and Cassie was thrown against the top of the trunk. Impulse had her jerking her arms to shield her head, but she couldn't get them in position with how they were bound. Instead she hit her head.

Wincing from the pain, she closed her eyes again. But not to go to sleep or to give up.

She needed to figure out a plan for when whoever had her opened up that trunk.

Because she had too much to live for to go down without a fight.

The car edged to a stop after another little while of driving. Cassie was hopeless enough measuring distances when she hadn't been unconscious for part of the time and left tied up in a trunk, so she didn't know how far they'd gone. Her head hurt and the accident itself was fuzzy in her head. She did remember heading up the road to the trailhead. The white car. Being tailed. She frowned.

The car that had been behind them had backed off, she remembered that. But she hadn't been completely relieved since she'd still felt like something was coming.

Sometimes she hated being right.

She heard footsteps crunching outside the car. Her heart rate sped up. She couldn't imagine seeing who'd been behind all this and her stomach churned at the idea of the terror they'd put her through, and the fact that they'd killed her aunt.

Unconsciousness couldn't be summoned though. So she had no choice but to face this.

The trunk opened and daylight spilled in. The light hurt her eyes.

Please, God, I'm not ready.

"Get out."

The voice was gruff, a male voice she didn't recognize. Somehow she'd assumed whoever killed her aunt was from Raven Pass, but this voice wasn't familiar to her. As soon as she had the thought, she remembered that a good portion of the rescue team had moved to Raven Pass after she'd left town. There were likely more newcomers also. Cassie not knowing who the man was didn't mean her aunt hadn't known him.

"My hands are tied so it's hard to move. Untie them."

The gruff laughter was void of any actual humor. "No."

Cassie kicked her feet forward to roll herself over as best she could, but finally the man reached in and grabbed her by the arms and lifted her out.

His strength scared her. She didn't want to die, but it would have been easier in the car crash. It terrified her to think of dying at the hands of someone with that much raw strength.

Her eyes still burning and dry, Cassie blinked against the daylight. They were in a parking lot, but not the one for the trailhead she and Jake had been heading to. "Where are we?"

"Near the gold. You're going to take us to it."

"We were heading to where we thought it was. You need to take me there. Of course, all that assumes I would actually help you find it." Neither honesty nor sarcasm were likely to hurt her at this point. At least she didn't think so. They'd already abducted her. It could only get worse if they had her son.

Fear stabbed her chest. She had to cooperate. If she didn't, they'd look for more ways to threaten her, and endangering Will wasn't an option. "Okay, I will show you. But truly, I don't know how to get there from here."

"You were going to a trailhead not far from here." His voice was low. Rough.

Cassie frowned. "I don't know where we are."

"Half a mile north of where you were going. Farther north on private property. Don't worry, your boyfriend won't look for you here. Neither will the police."

Any flicker of hope she might have entertained wavered, but didn't go out. She knew God now. And while she didn't know a lot about Him, she hoped maybe He would rescue her.

Right?

"Get me back on that trail and I'll see what I can do," Cassie said, hoping her voice stayed steady.

The big man nodded once.

Cassie started walking, her hands still behind her back, her heart beating hard and her mind trying to figure out how she was going to get out of this.

FOURTEEN

Jake's head hurt, throbbed with pain. He blinked himself back into consciousness, thinking in a detached way as he did so that getting what was likely a concussion two days in a row wasn't helpful to his brain.

When he was finally awake enough to panic, he looked to the passenger seat. No Cassie.

The police pulled up behind him just then, and Judah Wicks got out of his car.

Someone had called them? Jake certainly hadn't.

Judah Wicks walked over to him, talked to him about the accident while his head throbbed in pain. Was Jake hurt? Yes. Where was Cassie? Jake didn't know. He answered the questions like it wasn't him talking, like he was somewhere outside himself absentmindedly wondering if this was what utter panic felt like.

She wasn't with him, and the people who had taken her had already committed one murder.

God, please keep her safe.

Jake made himself focus until Judah drove away, after assuring him they'd look for Cassie. Judah had wanted to get Jake medical attention, but he'd deferred, told the man he'd take care of it himself.

After a deep breath, he put the key back in his dented but still functional car and got ready to drive.

They had a head start on him, but Jake wasn't going to quit until he found Cassie.

First though, he needed help. His mind was fuzzy, but that much was clear.

Jake opened his group text and texted his search-and-rescue group. Cassie's been taken. Meet at the trailhead from three days ago. Then he texted Officer Thomas, the man who had Will, and updated him in case the danger had heightened for his son in some way. He was relieved to receive a text back from him almost immediately. Will was fine, having fun, and Jake didn't need to worry about it.

Something he was finding out as a father—it was nearly impossible not to worry about your kid.

His phone rang. Not Cassie, saying she'd wandered off after their accident and was fine. Not even an unknown number that could be the start to finding out where she was and getting her back.

It was Adriana. Jake slid the phone icon to answer. "Did you get my text?"

"Yes. I'm on my way to you with Babe and he's ready to find her. Do you have something of hers he could smell to establish her scent?"

"I can find something." His car smelled like her. Half his house smelled like her. Cassie's presence was everywhere in his life and had been for days. And now she was gone. He had to make himself focus, and only did so by reminding himself that Cassie was counting on him right now.

"We're going to find her, Jake."

Adriana's voice was confident. Firm.

He nodded even though she couldn't see him, not sure if he believed her or not.

"Did you hear me? We are going to find her. I'll see you at the trailhead, Jake. And bring your A game. This team needs everyone and that means you can't be distracted right now with imagining what might have happened to Cassie in some made-up, worst-case scenario, okay? If you love Cassie, and I know you do, bring the Jake I know who is ready to handle this. Not this shell of a guy and not the cautious guy from the last few days. Bring my boss, okay?"

She hung up before he could tell her that basically everything she'd said was technically insubordination on some level. Or before he could say thank-you.

He exhaled.

God, even my realizing she didn't believe in You was halfway a relief. God, it gave me a chance to step back emotionally, since I want the woman I marry to know You like I do. But I do love her, God. I'm still waiting for her to trust You because I want to obey You in who I commit my life to, but Lord, if she ever does, she's the woman I want to marry. I don't want to be afraid of loving her again, or afraid of trusting, or of anything else. Please keep her safe, help her to trust You, and bring her back to me.

Please.

Jake took another breath, then lifted his head and put the car in gear, then gunned it to the trailhead, gravel kicking out behind his tires as he started.

By the time he got there, the rest of his team was already assembled and waiting. Several members of the Raven Pass Police Department were there too. Levi

Wicks and his brother Judah, Christy Ames, and another man Jake didn't recognize.

"Where do we search? Do you have quadrants in mind?" Ellie asked.

He shook his head. "It's going to be really unusual." He looked at Adriana. "I still want you to search with your dog like you usually would. If my plan goes against the dog's nose, go with his nose, okay?"

She nodded.

"The rest of you, Cassie knows where the treasure is, approximately."

"Uh, Boss, what treasure?" Piper raised her eyebrows. "Wait…" She frowned.

"The treasure in the legend people talk about?" Caleb finished for her.

Jake nodded. "Sorry, I forgot I didn't start at the beginning." Adriana had told him they needed him as their boss, and he needed to get it the rest of the way together. "Cassie figured out what her aunt knew that was worth killing over. She knew how to get to where the rumored Raven Pass treasure was buried, or hidden, we aren't quite sure which. There was an old fairy tale she told her that had directions in it."

He opened his phone to photos, where he'd taken a screenshot of the story as Cassie had written it down for him last night, then texted it to the group. "We're assuming this is the starting place. That's the assumption Cassie will be acting on."

"You think they took her to show them where the treasure is?"

Jake nodded. "Yes, because I believe that's why her aunt Mabel was abducted also."

Adriana frowned. "Then why kill her?"

"Maybe she wouldn't show them." Ellie shrugged. "I wouldn't."

"Your life is more important than that, just for the record," Jake said to her and everyone else, hoping Cassie understood that too. Why *hadn't* Mabel told them though? Jake hadn't figured that out. She would have known that she was more important also.

Please don't let Cassie make the same mistake.

"So does everyone understand our objective? Find Cassie." He hesitated, realizing for the first time the danger he'd be putting his team in. Cassie was clouding his vision. *God, help me see clearly.* "But..." He trailed off. "I understand if some of you want to bow out of this search. Your position on the search-and-rescue team won't be affected as today is outside the realm of our normal operations."

"We're coming, Boss. Now stop talking and let's go find your girl." Adriana started off first, Judah Wicks at her heels. Jake appreciated seeing the law enforcement officers spread themselves out among the search-and-rescue team so no searchers were without an officer and his or her weapon to protect them.

They followed the directions past the throne, but the trail all but disappeared. The directions from there were vague until wherever *the heart of darkness* was, Jake noticed when he looked at the story again. True north meant to go north. They'd have to cross at least one river, maybe two, or the same river more than once. He wasn't sure quite how literally to take the words.

"We should split up," Levi finally said after the group had started down several trails only to turn back when they became impossible to navigate.

"Fanning out will make it possible to cover more

ground anyway, and potentially approach a dangerous situation from multiple sides," his brother Judah spoke up.

Jake considered it and nodded. "Okay. No groups without an officer?"

Levi nodded.

Levi stayed with Jake. Judah went with Adriana. Christy went with Piper and Caleb. The other officer, whose first name he'd learned was Luke, was paired up with Ellie.

The woods seemed quiet after they split. Initially Jake could hear some of the noise from other groups, but then nothing. His heart thudded even harder in his chest. Someone was going to find her. He believed that. They'd assembled too good a team not to, especially when they had an idea of where her captors would most likely be headed. The question wasn't that. It was whether or not she'd be alive when they got there.

"Where did they park, Jake? If they took this trail?" Levi spoke up and Jake stopped in his tracks. The thought caught him that off guard. The black SUV that had hit him hadn't been in the lot and neither had the white car. Had another car been working with them? There had been several other cars.

"Do you think there's a third car involved?"

Levi shook his head. "I don't know what to think. It's possible but it's a lot more logical they parked somewhere else."

"Where else is there?" Jake asked as he was already pulling up the satellite view he'd looked at with Cassie the night before. He could barely think back to that, it hurt too much to think of the note on which they'd ended. Still, he studied the landscape. Levi leaned in too and both of them stared.

They saw it at the same time; Jake could tell by the way Levi tensed.

"There. What is that?" Jake asked.

"I'm not sure." Levi was staring at the same narrow road through the trees that showed on the satellite. It wasn't large enough to be any kind of official trailhead parking. But it was north of where they were, well within a mile. It was possible they intended to have Cassie take them to try to find the gold but didn't want to risk using this trailhead. They had to have known that as soon as Jake regained consciousness he'd come after her.

Which raised the question—why hadn't they killed Jake? Had they assumed the accident had done it? Had they not had time…

"Who called in the wreck earlier, do you know?" Jake asked his friend.

Levi shook his head. "Judah said it was a guy who saw it happen. He called it in and one of the other officers talked to him in person and took his statement."

That made sense. Jake hadn't understood why the guys who had caused the wreck hadn't finished the job with him when they were taking Cassie away, but if someone was there at the scene and saw it happen, murder was a bit harder to get away with.

"The witness saw them take Cassie away. How was she?"

Levi shook his head. "Unconscious, not responsive. We don't know anything else yet, so let's not speculate, okay?"

Jake forced himself to think about other things, things that weren't Cassie's limp body, maybe alive maybe not, being carried away from him. He'd promised to keep her safe and he'd failed at that. How was he supposed to forgive himself if he didn't get her back?

Summoning all the courage he still possessed, Jake nodded and glanced back at the satellite map. "It's a long shot, but let's head in the direction of the spot we noticed on the satellite."

"You think they parked there and came this way?"

"I'm almost sure of it."

"Let's go."

It was ironic, really, how one of the activities Cassie had loved to do with her aunt had factored into this week back in Raven Pass to such a great degree. Here she was, hiking again. Without her aunt, but here in town because of her aunt. Wondering if what had happened to her aunt was about to happen to her.

It felt eerily like walking in someone else's shoes as she walked down the trail. She was grateful she'd dressed in light long sleeves and long pants. It was unusually warm for Alaska, in the high seventies she'd guess, but the trail was overgrown, barely able to be called a trail from the place where the man who'd abducted her had parked. The branches of the trees scraped against her and the fabric kept them from scratching her skin.

As she walked, she felt oddly calm, whether from shock or from God kind of cushioning the emotional blows she should be feeling, Cassie wasn't sure. She knew though, that she felt strangely confident. The treasure was in these mountains and she knew how to get to it. Roughly. And she would find it and let them have it if it meant they would let her go.

No, she amended as she pushed through the branches

of several spruce trees that had grown together, it wouldn't mean they'd let her go. She wasn't naive enough to think it would. But it might be possible for her to get away from them when they were distracted by the gold.

Cassie wished she knew more about what it was supposed to look like. Were they talking gold nuggets, basically? She assumed so from the talk she'd heard occasionally around town and what she read in the book yesterday. The story seemed to imply that the gold had been hidden straight from the mountain, not processed in any way. So it might not be a stunning sight even if it was worth a substantial amount of money. She'd have to be ready to create her own sort of diversion if the gold itself wasn't enough to distract them into complacency.

"Speed up."

The harsh voice of her captor behind her startled her forward and she tripped on one of the rocks. A hand wrapped around her arm almost instantly, jerking her back to a standing position. It was a stark contrast to how she felt when Jake helped her, when his hand was on her arm.

She'd thrown away more than she'd known years ago. But she wasn't giving up on getting him back yet. If the faith issue had been the only one between them, that was solved now. If it had only been an excuse and he really hadn't forgiven her, or he just didn't love her anymore… Well those were possibilities but she would cross those bridges if and when she came to them.

Thinking about him now wasn't helping though. Her focus needed to be on the treasure and getting there as quickly as she could, as it appeared her captor was getting impatient. She had been walking at a slower pace than usual, thinking that the extra time to think might help her tactically somehow. He'd noticed and now she felt like he was watching her more carefully, so that had been a risk that hadn't paid off.

"Let's go."

The muscles in her legs were burning—there was nothing false about her pace now, she truly couldn't hike much faster. She forced herself to though, needing not to enrage him to the point that he hurt her or lost his temper. The man looked like he could crush her without much effort.

Help me, God. I want to get back to Will. And Jake, if he'll have me.

She prayed, that sentiment and more like it, as she pushed herself down the trail. When they reached a river, she looked back at the big man. He just stared at her. "Is it across the river?" he asked.

Cassie nodded.

"Then cross it."

There was no rope, nothing to aid her across the river. Except farther downstream there was a branch that overhung the water a little, and that might possibly be used to hang onto during the crossing. Cassie walked down that way on the gravel bank and discarded that plan. The branch was barely hanging onto the tree and could fall off any moment, and the water was deeper at that part of the river, swirling into eddies.

She walked back to where she'd been at first, thinking the shallower part might be easier.

"Do you have a preference where we cross?" she asked the man. He shook his head, then gestured with his meaty hand. "Just cross it."

His voice was rough. Hard.

And getting swept away in the current was prefer-

able to being at his mercy. Cassie felt her eyes widen
at the thought and she looked down immediately, then
looked back at the river, trying to appear natural when
so many thoughts were swirling in her head so fast, the
current of them almost as powerful and dangerous as
the river itself.

She was facing an impossible choice, she realized. But
she did have a choice. Option number one meant trusting that her captor would have some degree of honor, or
decency, and not kill her the moment she showed him
where the gold was. All of that assumed she could stay
alive long enough to do that. It felt like his temper was
on a hair trigger and at any moment he might explode
and that would be the end for her.

Had her aunt died that way? Violently and suddenly?
Cassie wanted to know, and didn't.

She swallowed hard and blinked back tears.

Option two meant surrender to God, and hope, and
everything that Cassie wasn't good at. Add to that the
practical aspect of surviving in the frigid water. A decade ago she'd been trained for wilderness situations by
her daily activities in Alaska. She'd grown soft working
in Florida, in a climate-controlled office and far from the
dangers and adventures of the backcountry. Just crossing the river would be much more difficult for her now.
She knew well that the temperature was enough to give
someone hypothermia if they spent much more than a
few minutes in it. And as a nurse, she understood hypothermia better than most. It was a fairly peaceful way
to die, if one had to make choices about things like that,
but it was unforgiving. Once you started down its road,
it seldom let someone turn back without medical intervention, and by virtue of what she was considering and

the danger she was in, medical intervention would not be an option, maybe for hours.

Still. It was her only hope. And if hope wasn't worth holding onto…what else was there?

Cassie walked back to the tree trunk. "I'm going to use the tree."

The big man nodded, folded his arms across his chest. It seemed he was willing to use her as a guinea pig and then decide his own route based on the one she took. The spinelessness of a man who would be willing to sacrifice a woman for his own safety or gain made her sick. She wanted to tell him that, that he made her want to throw up, but in case her plan didn't work and they ended up back together, she'd better not antagonize him.

The first step into the water was the coldest, and Cassie stepped back out immediately, her gasp reflex making her inhale sharply. She took a deep slow breath and tried again, letting the water rush over her hiking boots and soak through. Then she reached for the tree branch, her hands tightening around the wood of the branch itself, the leaves tickling her forearm. She took another step deeper into the river with her left foot, then her right. The water was above her ankles now. Cold, it was so cold. Her hiking pants soaked in the water and it crawled up her leg. The tree branch held. She continued across, the water now past her knees. On her thighs. She had to squeeze her eyes shut for a second and grasp for all her courage again because the cold made her want to cry. But she had to get across, or let herself be swept away.

Or…could she cross the river without him and manage to hide out somewhere? Cassie hadn't considered that option, but now she saw there was a chance. Probably not much of one if she let herself be swept away in the river, but it was an option and possibly safer than...

The branch snapped, the swirl of glacial blue water tugged harder against her, and Cassie felt herself being pulled down, into the churning water, and downstream.

Cold. That was the thought first and foremost on her mind. The water was ice cold like a thousand sharp icicles puncturing her skin all at once, all over. She heard herself screaming and then forced her mouth to close as she passed the man who was running into the water after her. She was his living map, she knew, and he wasn't likely to go without trying to get her back.

The thought was terrifying.

The current swept her farther downstream, around a curve, and when she was out of his sight, Cassie started to fight the water with her arms, desperate to gain buoyancy and get herself to the shore, where she could hide. She cupped her hands together and pulled the water with even strokes, slowing her breathing so she didn't panic. She was five feet away from the shore. Four feet.

She paddled harder. The current tugged her back out.

She wouldn't have much time in this water, she knew. That's why the entire plan had been a gamble.

Please let it have been a smart one.

The shore was closer now and she swam again, against the tug of the water. One more chance. She had what she guessed was one more chance before the cold and exhaustion would team up against her, bullies that they were, and prevent her from reaching the shore safely.

Everything depended on this next try.

Cassie swam hard, and she swam not just for her, or

for Will, or even Jake, but for hope and for the new life she had now that she'd trusted God.

See? I'm trusting You now, God, so please come through for me.

Her hands reached out and she grabbed another branch. It was thin, but it was flexible, and it held long enough for her to stand up in the thigh-deep water and pull herself the rest of the way to the edge with hesitant steps.

The first step on shore, Cassie almost cried. She'd made it, but she wasn't safe yet, couldn't rest yet. Instead of collapsing there, Cassie walked inland some, into a thick cluster of fireweed, and curled up in a ball. She had to stay warm. But she couldn't build a fire, not without being detected. Instead she prayed the sun was enough to keep her warm, and tried to stay awake.

But she couldn't. She fell asleep with a prayer on her mind, hoping she wasn't foolish to, for once in her life, trust and hope and wait.

FIFTEEN

Using the story Cassie had written out, as well as the satellite map, had gotten Jake and Levi halfway to where the treasure supposedly was from the trailhead, at least according to his entirely unscientific estimation. They were standing now at a riverbank, staring at the glacial river. It wasn't the largest Jake had ever seen, but it was silty and fast and that made it dangerous.

"You're sure you want to cross this?" Levi asked from a few feet away where he'd been looking out, trying to find a good path across the water. Some river crossings on hiking trails in Alaska would have ropes stretched across them, to help hikers get over them safely. Even with the ropes, it wasn't rare for someone to be pulled down by the current, held under by the heaviness of the silt, and then drowned. It was even more likely here without anything to aid in the crossing. Most Alaskan rivers were angry churning blue, filled with rocks that dared someone to not take them seriously, and offered death as a consequence of carelessness.

This one fit that profile. And Jake had too much to live for to die right now. But the story had said to cross the rivers they encountered. He pulled the wrinkled paper from his pocket, the one Cassie had written last night in her own handwriting.

"He was not stopped by rivers," Jake read aloud, then shrugged. "It sure sounds like we are supposed to cross it. It doesn't say to turn around or find another path."

"And you're sure this story really means something and is going to lead us to gold?"

Levi was trying to believe him and be supportive, Jake could tell, but he still wasn't sold on the idea, as Jake had known he wouldn't be. It was beyond their usual encounters with criminals, most of whom knew what they wanted. They were dealing with something unknown here, a legend. While Jake believed he and Cassie were right about their theories, he understood Levi's hesitation.

"I'm sure, but besides that, Cassie is sure. She'll follow what the story says."

"So we have to cross."

Jake nodded. He walked up and down the bank, trying to figure out where Cassie would have gone and if she'd have made it. Because the gold wasn't the point, and the men who had been after her weren't even the point for Jake. He would rather find Cassie safe, and if she hadn't made it across all the way…

"Do you think she would have made it—if she crossed this?" he forced himself to ask his friend, not sure he wanted to hear the answer.

Levi looked out again, then spoke up over the roar of the river. "I don't know. It's an intense current and she's been gone for a long time. You think she could do something like this?"

"She could if it wasn't too deep." Cassie was strong, Jake knew, but once water was over someone's knees, their strength started to make less and less of a difference. It was simple science as far as how deep someone could go before being overpowered. If the water was too deep, she wouldn't have stood a chance. Which meant if she had crossed, she should have done it right about where they were standing, in the middle of this clearing, straight across.

Still…he didn't see footprints. Would he see some between the rocks, on actual soil?

Maybe. He walked the river again, this time more toward his right. A tree branch overhung the water by about a foot or two, the end of it snapped like it had broken clean off the rest of itself.

Surely…

Cassie would have known better than to cross here, right? he asked himself as he looked down at the deeper water. Using the tree branch as a way across would have been tempting, especially with her having had experience crossing rivers with rope before. She would have defaulted to the way she knew how to cross safely and that was with something to hold onto. But the river here was deeper and the current angrier than in the other locations. If the tree had broken…the water would have been up to her waist, Jake was guessing. Far too deep for her to stand and hold her ground against the flow if she'd lost her handholds.

How long ago had the tree broken? Jake wished he'd studied something that would answer that question for him, instead of being a paramedic and having only worst-case scenarios for Cassie scroll through his mind. Mindless facts he'd once memorized, about drownings and water in the lungs, and the evidence of drownings in autopsies—those were the things he was thinking about now, and pondering them in conjunction with Cassie wasn't something he wanted to do. They weren't helpful, and he needed to do something to help. For years he felt like he'd let her down by not coming after her. He'd let his own fears, his own desire to be wanted and not rejected keep him from trying to get her back, and he'd learned. Maybe too late, but he had learned.

She was worth fighting for. And if her lack of belief in God was all there was between them… Jake would keep loving her and pray every day that she came to know the truth. He would try harder to be an example of a good Christian, to show her what it meant to be a person of faith. He would try to gently lead her, not pressure her. But he would not, could not give up on her again.

"She crossed here," he mumbled, knowing the truth clear down to his soul. He bent down to study the dirt. There, the slightest impressions of the soles of someone's shoes.

He heard noise behind him and turned his head. Levi.

"Did you find something?" Levi asked.

Jake nodded. "She crossed here."

His friend's eyebrows rose. "Because of the tree? You think it went farther out and then…"

Jake shook his head. "No way to know for sure. But I think she went here for some reason."

"If she was trying to escape someone, would she take her chances being swept down the river?" Levi asked.

Jake didn't know. Cassie wasn't a huge risk taker, and she'd struck him as even more careful now, since having Will. But if it was the only chance she'd had to escape, he knew she was brave enough to have taken it.

"Maybe," he answered.

"So do we cross? Or do we go downstream, hoping to find her?"

Jake struggled for an answer. "If she did go down the river, we still don't know which bank she'd have ended up on. She wants to know who killed her aunt. Would she have made an effort to cross?"

Levi didn't answer and Jake hadn't really expected him to. No one knew her as well as he did, and if he was asking questions, then so was everyone else.

All he could do was search all the options. "Let's start with this side, go downstream a bit and see what we can find," he said to Levi.

The other man nodded. "Okay. I'll update the other officers with our general position in case we run into trouble."

"Or..." Jake trailed off. "We could split up?"

Levi shook his head. "No. I've seen how that movie ends."

Jake laughed, appreciating the bit of humor. It was a good coping mechanism, lightening the mood. "Thanks. Okay, we'll go together. Downstream."

The brush was thick, and bushes grew along the river-bank that Jake didn't know enough about to identify, but there were several different kinds, of varying heights. The advantage was that if she'd come out of the river at any point, they should be able to see evidence in the trampled brush. So far, there was none of that right next to the river, or ahead of them either, which meant that no one had pursued her, at least on this side of the river.

Not a complete reassurance that they didn't have to be on guard, but it did make Jake breathe a bit easier. Someone was still out here, he knew, but maybe not in the immediate vicinity.

He said as much to Levi and Levi shook his head. "If someone was tracking her and walked through the river, right along the edge, we'd see no evidence."

Which meant the man who'd taken Cassie could be anywhere. Jake's small bit of hope disappeared again.

Finally, it occurred to him to pray. Ironic that he'd pushed Cassie away because of her lack of trust in God. But when it came down to it, did he trust God either? Not as much as he wanted to, that was for sure. He was an imperfect man who could only keep trying to do better every day.

Forgive me, God, for not asking earlier, and please help me. I don't want to give up hope. Please.

They continued on, each step in the spongy ground too slow. Neither of them wanted to end up in the river by accident, so it was slow going. Every minute that passed was a minute Cassie might be in danger, and Jake hated knowing that.

"Did you hear that?" Levi asked.

Jake hadn't. He stopped.

Something rustled in the bushes. Up ahead, off the riverbank about twenty feet. Would she have taken shelter so far away from the river?

Or was it whoever had abducted her in the first place, lying in wait?

Or burying a body?

Jake worried his heart would stop at the last thought. Not another one he was going to let himself have again. No, he was trusting, remember? Trying to hope.

So he called out her name. "Cassie?"

The rustling stopped. He held his breath.

"Jake?"

Her voice was watery, weak, and every thought he'd

had earlier about hypothermia and the dangers of the river came back to him. Jake fought again against the threatening feeling of hopelessness, knowing that with God there was always a chance. Never a reason to doubt. Always hope.

"Cassie!" he called again louder, hoping she'd answer so he could pinpoint exactly where she was. Beside him, Levi was looking around too, scanning the area for Cassie and for threats, Jake guessed.

"Here."

He saw the fireweed waving ahead of him, moving just enough to give it away as her location and he walked there. Levi came with him, but hung back slightly, which Jake appreciated. He wanted to see her first, know how she was, and he was desperate to know if she was all right.

She was, and she wasn't.

She was curled in a ball on the ground, the fireweed surrounding her like a tall curtain that came up from the ground. She'd been protected from being found by whoever had been after her, probably because she'd been so far off the river, and not on any obvious trail. Her choice of location had likely saved her life, and Jake thanked God for the intelligence he'd given Cassie so she could make that choice.

But while physically unharmed, she was soaked through—her clothes clung to her and her hair was wet too. She must have been pulled all the way under in her fight with the water.

This though, this he could handle. He wished he had equipment, but he could assess her at least, knew the signs of hypothermia, and no longer felt entirely helpless. A small mercy.

"How are you feeling?" He kept his voice even, reminding himself that if there'd ever been a time for professional detachment, this was it.

"I'm okay…" She sighed. "Sleepy. Just sleepy."

She wasn't shivering. That alarmed Jake. It was a warm day and the sun was out, which would help her, but there was a little bit of a breeze. Maybe she'd been protected from it enough by the fireweed, but he still had concerns. She needed to dry out.

"We need to get you warm, okay?"

"I can't…clothes are wet…"

Jake heard the slight slurring in her words that time and knew he'd been right to be concerned. They were there in time, but they had to act.

Building a fire could give away their location to anyone who was after her. He knew Levi had a weapon and more than enough training to use it. While Jake wasn't law enforcement, he'd grown up in the Alaskan woods and knew how to use a gun as well and had his own for bear protection. They were covered where that was concerned, but it wasn't enough to make him cocky about their chances. Bad guys could have guns too. It wasn't an automatic win for the good guys.

"How many men took you?" he asked her as he bent beside her to feel her pulse. It was fairly strong, better than expected. Jake breathed a prayer of thanks while he waited for her answer, continued to assess the situation. He removed his sweatshirt and tugged it over her head, instructing her to take off her wet shirt underneath. He turned around to give her privacy.

"Only one. I only saw one. He was so big." Her voice trailed off again. "I had to get away."

So he'd been right. She'd braved the river. Jake pulled

her toward him, did his best to hug her though the angle was awkward and she was half asleep. "You're going to be okay, all right? You've got this, Cassie."

"Not sure I do, but God does."

He stilled. Swallowed hard.

"What did you say?"

"God… I'm trusting, okay, Jake? But I need to sleep."

"No. No sleeping." Jake looked at Levi, who'd been standing by, waiting. He stood up, kept his words soft in case Cassie was still awake enough to listen. "We need a fire, like half an hour ago," he muttered.

Levi nodded. "I agree. She sounds hypothermic, right?"

Jake nodded.

"It's a risk," Levi said. "But everything is at this point. It seems worth it."

"How should we do this?" Jake knew the fire would make them more visible to anyone looking for Cassie. It was daylight, so no worries as far as the light giving them away, but the smell of smoke traveled on the wind and someone skilled in tracking would be able to pinpoint its general location.

"We'll just keep watching out, maybe take turns wandering around the site here, seeing if there's anything unusual." Levi shrugged. "That's all we can do while we wait for help."

Jake nodded. "Okay. I'm going to get some sticks for a fire." He glanced down at Levi. "You won't leave her?"

"I promise." Levi met his eyes and Jake knew his friend would watch her not just like anyone who needed police help, but like someone who was special to Jake.

When Cassie had left him in Raven Pass all those years ago, he'd tried to turn inward, back off from his friends. Instead God had kept pushing him to make new friends and he'd ended up with some of the best. Including Levi. Jake had to smile. "Thank you."

Levi nodded.

Jake wandered away and gathered the wood, alarm gathering in him when he didn't see Levi when he came back.

"Levi?"

Nothing.

"Cassie."

Nothing.

He couldn't remember where she'd been, not exactly. The scene reminded him so much of...yesterday? The day before? When they'd found her aunt Mabel's body and she'd hidden in some fireweed much like this. So much life had been crammed into the time between then and now, and yet this felt oddly like déjà vu.

Was she there, just unseen as she had been at first? Or had something far worse happened?

Levi being gone didn't bode well.

Jake kept looking around. He glanced at the fireweed, deciding he would try again there in a minute. He'd walk to the river now and make sure Levi hadn't gone down there, maybe even with Cassie.

He found Levi on the edge of the river, unconscious.

Jake gritted his teeth and bent beside his friend. His heart rate was good. Jake didn't see any bullet wounds, or any sign of head trauma. So either he'd been hit on the head or possibly drugged. He couldn't tell which without more assessments and tests, which he couldn't do out here.

Jake reached down and dragged him farther from the edge of the river. He'd gotten tangled in the branches of a small tree. Otherwise, he might have fallen in entirely. So he'd been…attacked and shoved toward the water? What had made the attacker leave?

Cassie? Could she have been awake enough to help? Jake wasn't sure. She'd been in bad shape.

He glanced at Levi again. Tugged him a little farther from the water.

"I'll be back. Sorry, buddy." He pulled Levi's phone out of his pocket and texted the police department to let them know their approximate location and that Levi needed help. Someone messaged back that they'd be coming.

One problem taken care of. Maybe two if they sent medical help along for Levi. They might come with supplies that could help Cassie too. Jake's knowledge wasn't much good without actual tools to put it into practice.

He hurried back to the fireweed.

"Cassie?"

Nothing.

He bent down on his knees, crawled through the bushes, sure she must be there. She'd fallen asleep, he told himself. He was just overlooking her hiding spot, which was good because it meant whoever had attacked Levi would have been unable to find her too.

He searched and searched. Found nothing.

And finally had to ask himself…why had Levi been so close to the river?

Jake had the sick feeling he'd let Cassie down again. This time though, he was going after her.

He ran toward the river, hoping he'd come up with a plan as he went.

She was so very tired. And cold. She was cold. Should she be cold, Cassie wondered, if she was hypothermic? She'd always understood hypothermia to be a warm death. Maybe then she wasn't dying.

At least not from hypothermia. She had many other options, sadly.

She looked across from her in the raft. The big man from earlier had been joined by another man, which was why they'd been able to overpower Levi before he'd even been able to get his weapon out. She'd felt sick as she watched the big one grab him in something like a head-lock and then drop him, shoving him toward the water as the other man pushed the raft with himself and Cassie in it out into the river. The big man had jumped in at the last minute and it was just the three of them. The two men had oars and were fighting the current to the other side, where they thought the gold was.

Her aunt. Maybe Levi. Maybe her next. And where was Jake? How many lives would be lost because of some gold? Did people's greed have no bounds?

It was something she wanted to learn about, if she lived. Why did God create people if they were going to be so messed up? She'd heard Jake mention the phrase *free will* but it wasn't something she understood. Maybe she never would.

Please help me get out of here. She tried to pray, but she was so tired. Tears crept into the corners of her eyes and everything in her was still even though the men were yelling at each other, the river seemed to be yelling at all of them, and even the weather was join-ing in as this morning's sunshine had been replaced by gathering clouds.

It had been too hot. Now a storm threatened. She could add lightning to the list of threats she was facing.

"Row harder!" the big man yelled at the other.

"I brought you the raft. I've done enough to help you, don't you think?"

"I said row harder!" His rage was growing, Cassie could feel it and it terrified her. She wanted to hide back in her cluster of fireweed, even though that would only be false security. After all, it hadn't kept her from being discovered earlier. The men had come soon after Jake had left, as if they'd been watching her the whole time.

"Row yourself!" the other yelled.

Cassie watched in horror as the big man hit the other with a paddle, so hard she saw the man's eyes roll back in his head as his arms flew backward, his body off balance, and then he fell over the backside of the raft into the river.

She looked at his lifeless body, tossing in the water, hitting the rocks, then back at the big man.

"Get his paddle and row."

Cassie did.

Fighting with terror and determination, she rowed as hard as she could. The river tossed them where it wanted, but eventually they were caught on a rock close enough to the other side that with some maneuvering, the big man was able to lean over and propel them to shore using his paddle as a pole.

"Get out," he ordered when they'd banged up onto the rocky edge.

Cassie did.

She swallowed hard. Eventually she was going to have to defy him if she wanted to live. His temper was a liability, one she could use against him, if she was smart.

And careful. She'd have to be very careful.

Cassie climbed out, feeling her heart beat in her chest, hard and strong and tired.

She was so very tired.

"Find. The. Treasure."

Cassie nodded, eyeing the clouds above them. She heard a rumble in the distance. If it rained, their footprints would be destroyed, and any chance of someone like Jake tracking them would be diminished. She couldn't afford to draw attention to herself enough to mark their trail in any other kind of way though. She'd seen what the big man's temper could do and she wasn't about to trigger it unless she could use it to her advantage.

Please let the rain hold off.

The bedtime story in her head, Cassie remembered they'd likely have to cross at least one more river. The story had said *rivers*. Was there another river? How big would this one be?

She found out before too long. It may have been a branch of the same river, or this may have been the confluence of two, Cassie wasn't sure. But there was another river, stretching in front of them.

"This time—" the man grabbed her arm again and she tried to hide her shudder "—we are going together."

Swallowing hard, Cassie nodded and they stepped into the water.

Her mind shouted alarms as they kept stepping deeper and the water crept up and up her legs. Muscle memory remembered falling, the feel of the swirling current pulling at her, throwing her into its swift downstream flow. Her chest tightened and breathing got harder. There was no real danger in crossing the river right now. So far the water was only at her knees. Easily crossed. Not a danger like the last crossing. They were in the middle of the river now, so the chances of it getting deeper were slim.

Help me, God. We can do this. Right? she asked, not expecting an answer, but she felt reassurance settle over her anyway, soul deep, in a way that bolstered her confidence even more.

Then they were out of the river, on rocky ground again.

"What next?" the man asked.

"We go north."

"And after that?"

"We have to go north first." Cassie tensed as she said the words, afraid the man would be angry she wouldn't answer him, but she'd understood all at once that if she gave him all the directions, he'd have no need of her. In order to keep herself useful, she had to leave him needing her.

For now, he seemed satisfied with that answer. Maybe it was the fact that she'd kept her tone soft and hadn't been forceful, or maybe God had helped her. Either way, Cassie was relieved. The landscape grew more and more treeless as they climbed higher up the mountain than they'd been earlier, winding through alpine tundra. It looked like an area that could have once held a successful gold mine. Cassie walked north, thankful for the survival and navigation classes she'd taken during her high school years.

The next phrase she thought was a directional clue. It had been *into the heart of darkness*, which she assumed meant some kind of cave. An opening into the mountain of some kind. Maybe even a mining tunnel?

She saw it up ahead, in the distance, but instead of relief at getting them to the right place, Cassie felt fear grip her, hard and unrelenting.

She was about to become superfluous. He'd need her for the directions through the tunnels that she suspected were inside the mountain and that the story referred to when it said *left, right, left, left*. But after that... Time was running out to make her escape or figure out another plan. Overpowering her captor was out of the question, but there had to be something she could do.

"See the mining tunnel?" Cassie gestured to it.

The man nodded. "It's in there?" He was breathing heavily, anticipation making him lean toward her in a way that was even more intimidating than before.

Cassie nodded, about to open her mouth to explain the mazes, so he'd know he still needed her. But she wasn't fast enough. She saw one big fist of his coming against her head and she was unconscious.

Jake kept the story out as he hiked, like it was a literal map that he could see points on, as he moved ahead. He'd crossed the second river now and was making his way north. Soon, if he'd gone the right way, he should see whatever was described as *the heart of darkness*.

Was Cassie inside yet, and even more importantly, had her abductor harmed her in any way? They'd want to see the gold before they killed her, at least Jake thought so. But Cassie had seemed terrified, not just hypothermic, when he'd found her. And for her to have braved the river's current rather than try to overpower her captor, the man must be terrifying. Because Jake knew Cassie, and the woman wasn't scared of much. That was part of why he loved her.

He walked the trail he felt sure she must have walked just a short while before and wondered if officers had made it to Levi yet. He hoped so. He knew his friend would feel awful when he woke up, but again, that was another reason for Jake to be reminded to take these men who had Cassie seriously. His friend was no easy man to overpower.

So far the rain had held off, for which Jake was thankful, but now he felt drops starting to fall, first on his arms, then on his head as they hit hard enough to feel through the baseball cap he wore.

There. He could barely see a dark spot on the mountainside up ahead, but it was enough to see it was likely the *darkness* described by the story. He hurried in that direction and came to a cave. Not a cave, a mining entrance. It was cool and dark, many degrees colder than the warmer air outside. Cassie's hypothermia came back to the forefront of his mind. She was battling more than one enemy and he could help her with neither right now. Jake hated being helpless.

The tunnel was so dark he couldn't see, and he didn't want to use a light and give away his presence. Jake stepped out again, back into the light where he could read the story on the paper.

"Left, right, left, left."

He could remember that. He stepped back into the darkness and crept forward. He put both hands out and decided it felt like a standard kind of mining tunnel, at least from the little he knew about them. It was about two feet wide, maybe less. Just enough for him to walk through, but passing someone would require flattening your body against one wall while they flattened theirs on the other. People were smaller in the 1930s so they'd likely made tunnels to fit how people were built back then. That also explained why he had to stoop a little; his over six-foot frame would have scraped the ceiling if he'd stood at his full height.

He kept going forward, not noticing any place where

he had the option to make any turns. The story indicated that there should be some. He'd just begun to wonder if he'd missed them at some juncture when he came to the first option. Straight or left.

Left.

He made the turn, followed a tunnel that felt identical as far as specs to the one he'd just left.

Another juncture, maybe five minutes later. Right.

At the next intersection, there were multiple ways to turn. Straight. Left. Right.

He turned left, remembering the story. And then he could hear voices. They were low, in the distance, but they echoed enough on the walls of the tunnel that he could make out some of the words.

One of the individuals was angry. A man. His voice was low and full, maybe the man who'd nabbed Cassie. Anther voice was higher pitched. Female.

And older. Familiar.

Jake frowned, struggled to place it. He'd heard it somewhere...

He crept closer, mindful of how sound echoed, and tried not to make any noise. He needed surprise on his side if he was going to help Cassie at all.

Even then, their odds weren't good. But he wasn't giving up.

Help us, God.

Jake held his breath, and kept walking.

SIXTEEN

Cassie heard them talking well before she opened her eyes. In fact, she kept her eyes shut longer than she should have, listening. Waiting to see what the situation was.

"We should have stayed at the entrance. You took her in before I got here, without my say so, and who knows where we are in this stupid cave. I told you we needed her for the directions!"

The voice was female. Familiar. Cassie kept listening. Then peeked her eyes open the slightest bit.

The man shrugged. "She stayed out longer than I expected."

"Because you're an ape who hits harder than you think. Don't think I didn't notice that Lowell is gone. I'm assuming you killed him too?" She made a noise of disgust. "Your habit of killing people whose help we still need is infuriating."

"You asked for my help."

His tone was growing deeper, more menacing. Cassie remembered the scene earlier, in the raft, and felt herself tensing, though she tried not to let her facial expression change. She was supposed to be unconscious.

And she had been when they got into the cave. But she'd woken up after her captor had taken the first left turn. He'd guessed correctly. The next turn he'd gone right. Simple human instinct, to vary your guesses. And he'd guessed right. But the next turn he'd gone right again. That's when he'd stopped and the woman had found him. From a tracker? She doubted cell phones got signals inside the mountain. Had she been waiting? No, if she'd known how to get there, they wouldn't have needed Cassie, or her aunt.

She must have been nearby. Or the big man must have stayed with Cassie outside the cave for as long as it took the woman to get there and the woman had followed them without Cassie hearing her voice till now? Cassie had faded in and out, maybe, during the first couple of turns.

So she had a guess as to where they were in relation to the treasure, but she wasn't sure. That put her at a disadvantage.

Her only current advantage was that they thought she was unconscious. She needed to keep that going as long as possible.

"I asked for your help and so far you've only hurt." The woman's voice was cold. Unfeeling.

Cassie felt the man's rage, heard it in the cry he let out, and then a gunshot exploded, its noise reverberating off the walls in an echo of piercing sound.

A huge thud. Cassie's eyes flew open, found the man in the light from several lamps that were lit nearby. He lay bleeding on the ground, eyes unseeing.

Dead.

A woman stood over him, maybe ten feet from Cassie.

They were in a wider spot of the cave, not narrow like most of the passages.

It was the librarian, Mrs. Carpenter.

"Hello, Cassie."

"You…" She trailed off, hating how stereotypical she sounded, but her thoughts clamored over each other. She couldn't think. This woman was old. Not that old, but too old to…

To what? Shoot people? Clearly not.

All her preconceived notions about the person she'd been running from were shattered; one of them was lying dead on the floor, bleeding out nearby, the tinny smell of his blood overwhelming her. *He* had been who she'd pictured when she lay in bed afraid at night. And while she knew she and Jake had seen a man at times, so it might have been the big man, or the man called Lowell, or both as at the library, this woman, from what Cassie had heard in the last few minutes, had been behind it all.

"Why…"

The woman shook her head. "No one should have had to die, Cassie, don't you see that?" Her voice was prim. Proper as well as aged. She was one of Raven Pass's citizens who'd been there the longest. Her family, Cassie's family and a couple of others, they'd been there at the beginning.

"Why, then? You killed my aunt." She hated the words as she said them, rage threatening her as she realized that physically, she could overtake this woman.

"Don't do it, dear. You'll only end up dead, and I still won't have my treasure, and we will all be unhappy, don't you see?"

"You…"

Mrs. Carpenter shook her head, the lamplight glit-

tering off her widened eyes. "I didn't do that. He did."
She gestured. Then shrugged. "I didn't mean for her to
die. I just wanted her scared enough that she would tell
me. That *brute*—" her tone turned disgusted "—ruined
that avenue and I was forced to look for other ways to
find the treasure."

"You took the books from her house," Cassie accused,
knowing without confirmation that she was right.

The woman nodded. "She always did take such good
notes in her books. But while the margins were filled
with confirmations of what I suspected, there were no
directions. So I had to get your help."

"I'm not helping you." Cassie folded her arms across
her chest. Waited while the older woman stared at her.

Even now, she struggled to believe this was the person who'd been after her, who was responsible for her
aunt's death.

Why? She had so many questions. She may as well
ask them now.

"How did you know about the notes?"

The woman's smile was nothing short of smug. "Your
aunt told me, dear! I'm a friendly sort, as the town librarian, and she would come in regularly to do geneal-
ogy research. That's what tipped me off to your family's
bad history."

Bad history?

She was curious about that too, but wasn't going to let
the woman get away with dodging her question. "Okay,
but what about the margin notes? You talked to her about
them?"

"I told her one day how some library patrons marked
up the books, and she said she only wrote in her own
personal books. I knew by then she was doing a lot of

digging on what had happened back in the day to the treasure. So I pressed her on that, and she revealed how she was taking notes about it in her own copies."

Cassie fully expected the gun to train on her then, but the woman's arms didn't move. She laughed a little, and it wasn't an evil sound like Cassie would have imagined. It was normal, light. Which made it even eerier.

"What did the books say in the margins?" Her curiosity was too great. And maybe the woman would answer, if she thought it would motivate Cassie. It wouldn't. But it was worth a try.

Her eyebrows raised. "You don't know? Surely she told you."

Cassie involuntarily shivered at the implication her aunt had kept things from her. But Cassie knew it was true. Hadn't they guessed her aunt knew where the treasure was? Of course there would have been other secrets tied to that, but if they didn't relate to Cassie, she hadn't needed to know. She couldn't be upset with her aunt for keeping that secret.

"Your family, Cassie. It's your family in the legend. They were the murderers."

She blinked, feeling the words like a slap across the face.

Mrs. Carpenter smiled, clearly pleased with her reaction. "See? So let's not be so hasty to judge here. People do nasty things for gold, Cassie. I'm no different than your relatives, the people you came from."

Cassie searched the statement for truth, struggled against it, fought to deny that her family had had anything to do with it, but she wasn't sure it wasn't true. They'd been there when the town was founded. Her aunt had reacted strangely to the treasure, kept it a secret and died refusing to give it up.

Had she been trying to make up for the wrongs that had been done by their relatives years before?

"So take me to it, dear. Like I said, I never wanted anyone to die." She shook her head.

Cassie stood, slowly.

Finding the treasure would at least give her closure, before she likely died. That was the worst-case scenario. Best-case was that someone found her here, that help arrived and she got to go free and Mrs. Carpenter spent the rest of her life in jail. The idea of the aristocratic lady behind bars was almost worth the terror.

But not worth the loss of her aunt. Not worth the heartbreak of knowing her family line had possibly done something so awful.

"This way," Cassie said and did her best to lead them back to where they could follow the directions of the story again, back to the entrance of the tunnel. She walked down the dark path, the light from the lantern Mrs. Carpenter carried giving her enough illumination to have shadows and shapes she could make out. Cassie wanted to cry. All these years she'd thought her mom was the worst of her family, and had been terrified she'd repeat her mistakes and leave the people she loved.

Then Cassie had done just that, in her effort to not repeat her mom's mistakes. She'd ironically done the same. What about these relatives? Was she destined to make their mistakes too? Not murder. Cassie was no killer. But betraying people for gold? Letting greed get the best of her?

God, who knows? Help me. Am I more than my history? Their history?

There in the tunnel, Cassie knew undoubtedly that she was not alone. God was with her. God was answering her, in her heart. Not in words but in steady reassurance.

No, she was not those relatives.

She was not her mom.

You are mine.

It was a Bible verse, part of one she remembered from a sermon she'd heard when she'd been dating Jake. From the Book of Isaiah, maybe?

She was God's. Not defined by any of that. But defined by Him. Cassie held her shoulders straighter. Kept walking, and begged God to help her, one more time.

The gunshot was the last straw. Jake could wait no longer. He crept toward the voices and was rewarded with the sight of Cassie. Her eyes were wide and she was talking to a woman. When the woman turned, Jake recognized her as the little old librarian.

People never stopped surprising him. Mostly in bad ways.

He watched them, listened and moved back into the shadows as they moved in his direction. They were close to the treasure, but not quite there and Cassie would be at a disadvantage, trying to find where they'd gotten off course.

He expected it to take a while for her to find it, but she made the turns well, like she'd been waiting for this all her life, and with the bedtime story, maybe she had been.

Good girl, Cassie.

The two women were ten feet in front of him, almost close enough to touch, but he was so careful not to make any noise that they hadn't heard him. There was a possibility the older woman couldn't hear well in her older age, which would work to his advantage.

"There," Cassie said and Jake crept as close as he dared.

He saw them both, leaning toward the tunnel wall. Not at the end, not in any obvious place, just a little notch out of the wall of the tunnel about as high up as a man would carve if he was reaching up but not to his full height.

Cassie reached up there, came down with first a slip of paper. He watched her facial expression flicker as she read it, and shoved it in her pocket.

Someone tapped Jake on the shoulder. He jumped. Levi. Judah. Adriana. Piper. Piper made the classic shh-signal with her hand.

Jake's face must have asked his questions because Piper pointed at Levi. He must have come to and led them there. Jake nodded, then waited, and all of them watched the scene in front of them.

"That's it? That's not the treasure, is it?" The woman raised a gun at Cassie. "Give it to me."

Jake made himself wait. If he hit her from this angle, the gun might discharge, killing Cassie.

"It's up there. That's a note to me."

The gun lowered.

"Get it down." The woman's voice was firmer now. Steely. "Actually… If it's there, then that means I don't need you anymore."

She raised the gun again. This time more purpose-fully. Levi tapped Jake, motioned for him to move left. Jake did.

"Freeze!" Levi yelled.

The woman whirled around, caught off guard.

"Raven Pass Police, put down your weapon!"

The librarian turned again to Cassie, gun at the ready.

Levi, Judah, someone, Jake didn't know, pulled the trigger.

The woman fell, hit somewhere center mass in the stomach. That threat was disabled. Cassie stood pressed against the opposite wall, having been less than two feet from the bullet and no doubt terrified.

Judah hurried toward the librarian, ready to perform first aid. Jake glanced at her as he rushed over to Cassie. Mrs. Carpenter might be going into shock, but Jake had a feeling she'd make it. Good. He'd rather see her live out her days in prison than die here. And he didn't want his friends to deal with the guilt of having had to end a life, though their shot had been justified.

But right now, Jake cared mostly about Cassie.

"Cassie." He reached for her and she came into his arms, wrapping hers around him and burying her face in his neck. Sobs racked her and he felt her tears soaking his shirt.

"She was behind it all along, Jake. How could someone do that? How could they be so greedy?" More sobs. "And the murders that started the legend? Apparently some relatives of mine did it. I don't understand. How could people do that?"

Jake didn't have answers for her questions, so he just held her until she ran out of tears.

"We're going to get her out. A helicopter is meeting us outside," Levi told Jake, motioning toward the injured woman.

Jake nodded.

"I want to get out of here," Cassie told him.

"Want to get the treasure first?"

She hesitated. "Can I…?" She sighed heavily. "Yes. I can do it."

He tilted his head, unsure of what she was thinking. She reached into her pocket and handed him the note he'd seen her pull down from the shelf that he assumed held the gold.

My Cassie,

If you find this, I'm likely gone. My apologies for handling this badly. I tried to tell you many times during your life, but the time never seemed right. You were always worried about becoming your mother, but you aren't her mistakes, dear. And you aren't our family's mistakes either.

The legend is true. There was a double murder, over some gold. But neither person who died was responsible. They were innocent, the ones who had found the gold. Your great-grandfather killed them, stole their gold.

He died not long after, in World War II, and never got to use the gold he'd stolen. He told his wife, who was racked with guilt. The story was passed down and rests now on me. One day, the hope was, someone in the family would be brave enough to return the gold to the town of Raven Pass. Neither man who died had a family so that gold is the town's. I almost brought it back. That's why I'm here in this cave today. But I can't do it, so instead I'm writing this note. If you find it, then possibly the paranoia I've had about someone asking me questions about the gold isn't paranoia at all. My life may be in dan-

ger, but, Cassie, even still I cannot find it within
me to just turn the gold in to the police. I can't
take people thinking ill of my dead family.

Be stronger than me, dear. If you find this, you
can find the gold. It's where this letter was. Do
the right thing, Cassie. Give it back. But let the-
comments roll off you. You aren't your relatives
or their mistakes. You aren't even your past, dear.
I love you. Forgive me, dear.
Mabel

Jake brushed a tear from his own cheek, his heart so
connected to Cassie's he felt he could feel her pain as
his own. "I'm sorry, sweetheart."

"She died doing what was right though." Cassie
sniffed. "In the end, she was braver than she thought."

Jake nodded. "She was, sweetheart. She was."

They walked together two feet forward, and Cassie
reached up, pulled a small box off the shelf and opened
it. Jake shined a flashlight down in.

Gold nuggets. Enough of them to be worth hundreds
of thousands now. Maybe more. His eyes widened.

"I'm going to give it to the town, Jake. I'm going to
do what she asked." Cassie nodded.

"And then?" Maybe it was the wrong time, but he
had to know. Was this going to push her away, make her
leave Alaska? Was there any hope at all?

"And then…if God wants me to, I thought I might
stay here. Raven Pass would be a wonderful place to
raise our son…" She trailed off. "And I'd like to raise
him with you."

"I would like that too, Cassie. Only one thing…" He
reached for her again, pulled her into his arms. He knew

sometimes men went down on one knee, and he'd done that before, but right now he just wanted to be as close to her as possible. "I want to marry you, Cassie Hawkins. I want to wake up next to you every day and know before God that our love is honoring Him. I want to raise Will with you and who knows how many other kids."

"I would like nothing better."

She lifted her face to his and he met her lips in a kiss. Long. Slow. Just enough of the past to remember that it had led them there.

But mostly, promise for the future.

EPILOGUE

The sun was shining and Cassie was dressed in white, ready to marry the man she should have married years ago. Then again, maybe it was good she hadn't. God had done so many things in her heart and taught her so much that she never would have learned otherwise. It was time, Cassie thought, to stop thinking about what she wished she could change about her past and start being thankful for the future.

At her side, Will tugged on the skirt of her dress. "Do I really have to wear a tie?" He made a face. His bowtie was lopsided, but he looked adorable in his suit. When she and Jake had gone home a month ago and told him that they were going to get married, he'd done a loud war whoop and run around the house like a crazy person. He'd come out of his shell so much in Raven Pass, partly from being around other boys his age outside of the school environment, and partly from the confidence that came from having his dad in his life, Cassie thought.

"You have to wear a tie." Cassie pulled him close and kissed his hair.

"Mom." He rubbed at the spot where she'd kissed

him, creating an even messier appearance than he'd had a minute ago. "No more kissing."

"I'm going to kiss your dad in just a few minutes, during the wedding," she reminded him, having done her best to explain how weddings worked the night before, since he'd had questions and had never been to one.

He wrinkled his face. "Kissing is gross."

She smiled. "Hey, buddy?"

He looked up at her.

"Thanks for being excited about our move. You're going to love it up here and I know your dad is so happy we will all be a family."

He nodded. "Uhh, me too, Mom. Can I go play now?"

That was what she got for expecting seriousness out of a six-year-old. Cassie laughed. "Not now, the ceremony is starting."

She heard the music that was their cue. Will was walking her down the aisle, toward his dad and their future. It had seemed appropriate, especially since he was the only family she had left.

They walked down the aisle and Cassie's eyes met Jake's. The way he looked at her, all love and warmth and faithfulness, was more than she could have dreamed or hoped for, but she'd learned in the past month of being a Christian that sometimes God works that way.

Thank you. Thank you so much, she prayed as she walked, one foot in front of the other.

"Dearly beloved, we are gathered here today to celebrate..." the pastor started, a nice man she'd met during hers and Jake's premarital counseling sessions the last few weeks, but all Cassie saw was Jake.

And in his face she saw forgiveness. She saw a future instead of a past. And she saw hope.

They repeated their vows and he held her hands and then finally, *finally*, it was official.

"You may kiss the bride."

Their lips met and inside Cassie's heart she knew she'd never felt as loved as she did right now. They kissed and kissed until there was laughter from the guests and then Cassie felt pulling on her dress again.

"That's about enough kissing," Will said dryly. "Come on, someone told me we get cake now!"

Cassie and Jake laughed, and he took her arm in his, then they walked together, as a family, out of the church and into their new life.

Together.

* * * * *

Dear Reader,

Thank you for coming along to Raven Pass and the first book in this series. This series was created while I was spending some time in the little town of Girdwood, Alaska, and got to thinking about what it would be like to set a book in that town, set in a forest among the mountains. *Alaskan Mountain Murder* is a result of that and I'm so excited it's out now and in your hands!

In this book, Cassie and Jake struggle with their past choices and how those have impacted the future. They wrestle with how to trust each other again, and Cassie in particular wrestles with her faith in God.

Have you ever felt like it was too late for God to use your past? Or like because you'd made some poor choices God couldn't redeem your past? God is in the business of making beautiful things from situations in which we aren't sure how to find Him. I hope this book reminds you of that.

I love to hear from my readers! You can find me online at facebook.com/sarahvarlandauthor, or send me an email at sarahvarland@gmail.com. Thank you so much for reading this book and for supporting authors in general. We couldn't do what we do without you.

Sarah Varland

COMING NEXT MONTH FROM
Love Inspired Suspense

Available June 2, 2020

DEADLY CONNECTION
True Blue K-9 Unit: Brooklyn • by Lenora Worth
On her way to question US Marshal Emmett Gage about a DNA match that implicates someone in his family in a cold case tied to a recent murder, Brooklyn K-9 officer Belle Montera is attacked. Now she must team up with Emmett to find the killer...before she becomes the next victim.

PLAIN REFUGE
Amish Country Justice • by Dana R. Lynn
After overhearing an illegal gun deal, Sophie Larson's sure of two things: her uncle's a dangerous crime boss...and he wants her dead. With a mole in the police force and Sophie in danger, undercover cop Aiden Forster has no choice but to blow his cover and hide her deep in Amish country.

SECRETS RESURFACED
Roughwater Ranch Cowboys • by Dana Mentink
When new evidence surfaces that the man her ex-boyfriend's father was accused of drowning is still alive, private investigator Dory Winslow's determined to find him. But working with Chad Jaggert—the father of her secret daughter—wasn't part of her plan. Can they survive the treacherous truth about the past?

TEXAS TWIN ABDUCTION
Cowboy Lawmen • by Virginia Vaughan
Waking up in a bullet-ridden car with a bag of cash and a deputy insisting she's his ex, Ashlee Taylor has no memory of what happened—or of Lawson Avery. But he's the only one she trusts as they try to restore her memory...and find her missing twin.

STOLEN CHILD
by Jane M. Choate
On leave from his deployment, army ranger Grey Nighthorse must track down his kidnapped daughter. But when he's shot at as soon as his investigation begins, he needs backup. And hiring former FBI agent Rachel Martin is his best chance at staying alive long enough to recover his little girl.

JUSTICE UNDERCOVER
by Connie Queen
Presumed-dead ex-US Marshal Kylie Stone goes undercover as a nanny for Texas Ranger Luke Dryden to find out who killed his sister—and the witness who'd been under Kylie's protection. But when someone tries to kidnap the twins in her care, she has to tell Luke the truth...and convince him to help her.

LOOK FOR THESE AND OTHER LOVE INSPIRED BOOKS WHEREVER BOOKS ARE SOLD, INCLUDING MOST BOOKSTORES, SUPERMARKETS, DISCOUNT STORES AND DRUGSTORES.

LISCNM0520